Nic let out a long, slow breath, rubbing his hand across the back of his neck.

For a minute Lily wondered if she'd completely misread what had been going on between them—maybe he was more interested in just being friends?

She risked a glance up at him and all her doubts fled. The heat in his eyes told her everything she needed to know about how he felt—and it was a lot more than friendly. She felt that heat travel to the depths of her belly, warming her from the inside until it reached her face as a smile.

He pulled gently on her hand, bringing her close to him, and planted his other hand on her hip.

'Is this a good idea?' she asked, knowing the answer, and knowing just as well that it wasn't going to stop them.

'Terrible,' Nic answered, dropping her hand, his palm finding her cheek. 'Want to stop?'

Stop? How could they stop? They'd tried to avoid it—they'd talked about exactly why it was a bad idea. Looking deep into Nic's eyes now, she could see that he still had reservations, that he still didn't fully believe this was the right thing to do…but stop?

'No.'

Dear Reader,

I've been living with Lily and Nic for a long time. This was one of the first stories that I tried to commit to paper, and over the years they have been through lots of changes—different jobs, different names and different locations. The one thing that hasn't changed over that time is their love and commitment to one another, and their love for the precious baby who lands so unexpectedly in their lives.

This book has been so much a part of my journey as a writer that's it's hard for me to believe it's finally here, in real book form, with a beautiful cover and the expertise of Mills & Boon® behind it. I owe a huge debt of gratitude to the many, many people who have helped me *and* the story reach this point.

It's my absolute privilege to present *Newborn on Her Doorstep*, and I only hope that Lily and Nic touch your hearts in the same way that they did mine all those years ago.

Love

Ellie

NEWBORN ON HER DOORSTEP

BY
ELLIE DARKINS

All rights reserved including the right of reproduction in whole
or in part in any form. This edition is published by arrangement with
Harlequin Books S.A.

This is a work of fiction. Names, characters, places, locations and
incidents are purely fictional and bear no relationship to any real
life individuals, living or dead, or to any actual places, business
establishments, locations, events or incidents. Any resemblance is
entirely coincidental.

This book is sold subject to the condition that it shall not, by way of
trade or otherwise, be lent, resold, hired out or otherwise circulated
without the prior consent of the publisher in any form of binding or
cover other than that in which it is published and without a similar
condition including this condition being imposed on the subsequent
purchaser.

® and TM are trademarks owned and used by the trademark owner
and/or its licensee. Trademarks marked with ® are registered with the
United Kingdom Patent Office and/or the Office for Harmonisation in
the Internal Market and in other countries.

Ellie Darkins spent her formative years devouring romance novels, and after completing her English degree she decided to make a living from her love of books. As a writer and editor her work now entails dreaming up romantic proposals, hot dates with alpha males and trips to the past with dashing heroes. When she's not working she can usually be found at her local library or out for a run.

Books by Ellie Darkins

Mills & Boon® Romance

Frozen Heart, Melting Kiss
Bound by a Baby Bump

Visit the author profile page at
millsandboon.co.uk for more titles

MORAY COUNCIL LIBRARIES & INFO.SERVICES	
20 39 62 22	
Askews & Holts	
RF RF	

For Rosie and Lucy

CHAPTER ONE

LILY TUCKED HER pencil behind her ear as she headed for the door. She almost had this website design finished, with a whole day to go before the client's deadline. She was privately amazed that she'd managed to get the thing done on time, given the chaos in her house. Even now she could hear chisels and hammers and God knew what else in her kitchen, as the builders ripped out the old units ready for work on the extension to start.

The ring of the doorbell had been welcome, actually. When she'd glanced at her watch she'd realised that she'd not taken a break since settling down in her home office at six. She was overdue a cup of coffee— and no doubt the builders would appreciate one, too.

A glance through the hallway window afforded a glimpse of a taxi heading up the road, but she couldn't see anyone waiting behind the frosted glass of the front door. Strange… she thought as she turned the key and pulled the door open.

No one there.

Kids? she wondered, but she'd lived in this house almost all of her life, and she couldn't remember a single case of knock-door-run.

She was just about to shut the door and head back inside when a kitten-like mewl caught her attention and she glanced down.

Not a kitten.

A Moses basket was tucked into the corner of the porch, out of the spring breeze. Wrapped tight inside, with just eyes and the tip of a soft pink nose showing from the yellow blanket… A baby.

Lily dropped to her knees out of instinct, and scooped the baby up from the floor, nestling her against her shoulder. Making sure the blanket was tucked tight, she walked down to the front gate, looking left and right for any sign of someone who might have just left a baby on her doorstep.

Nothing.

She moved the baby into the crook of her arm as she tried to think, her brain struggling to catch up with this sudden appearance. And as she moved the baby she heard a papery crackle. When she pulled the corner of the blanket aside she found a scribbled note on a page torn from a notebook. The writing was as familiar as her own, and unmistakable.

Please look after her.

Which left all the questions she already had unanswered and asked a million more.

She walked again to the gate, wondering if she could still catch sight of that taxi—if she had time to run and stop her half-sister before she did something irreversible. But as much as she strained her eyes, the car was gone.

She stood paralysed with shock for a moment on

the front path, unsure whether to run for help or to take the baby inside. What sort of trouble would her half-sister have to be in to do this? Was she leaving her here forever? Or was she going to turn up in a few minutes and explain?

For the first time Lily took a deep breath, looked down into the clear blue eyes of her little niece—and fell instantly in love.

His feet pounded the footpath hard, driving out thought, emotion, reason. All he knew was the rhythm of his shoes on the ground, the steady in-out of his breath as he let his legs and his lungs settle in to their pace.

The sun was drying the dew on the grassy verges by the road, and the last few commuters were making their way into the tube station. The morning commute was a small price to pay to live in this quiet, leafy part of London, he guessed.

He noted these things objectively, as he did the admiring looks from a couple of women he passed. But none of it mattered to him. This was the one time of the day when he could just concentrate on something he was completely in control of. So, no music, no stopping for admiring glances—just him and the road. Nothing could spoil the hour he spent shutting out the horrors of the world—great and small—that he had encountered in his work over the years.

Tomorrow he'd be able to find a solitary path through the Richmond Park, but this morning he was dodging café tables and pedestrians as he watched the street names, looking out for the address his sister had texted to him. She'd been taking furniture deliveries for him before he flew home, and had left the keys to his new place with a friend of hers who worked from home.

He turned the corner into a quiet side street, and suddenly the fierce cry of a newborn baby ahead skewed his consciousness and he stumbled, his toe somehow finding a crack in the footpath.

He tried to keep running for a few strides, to ignore the sound, but found it was impossible. Instead he concentrated on counting the house numbers—anything to keep his mind off the wailing infant. But as the numbers climbed he felt a sense of growing inevitability. The closer he drew to the sound of the baby, the more he wished that he could get away—and the more certain he became that he wouldn't be able to.

The rhythm and focus that had always come as easily as breathing when he pulled on his running shoes was gone. His body fought him, sending awareness of the baby to his ears. Another side street loomed on his left, and for a moment he willed himself to turn away, to *run* away, but his feet wouldn't obey. Instead they picked up their pace and carried straight on, towards a dazed-looking woman and the wailing baby standing in the porch of one of the houses ahead.

He glanced at the house number and knew that he'd been right. His sister had sent him to a house with a baby—without a word of warning.

'Hi,' he said to the woman, approaching and speaking with caution. Lily, he thought her name was. 'Is everything okay?' He couldn't help but ask—not when she was standing there with a distressed baby and looking as if she'd just been thunderstruck.

Her blonde hair was pulled back into a loose ponytail so shiny that he could almost feel the warmth of the sunlight reflecting off it. Her eyes were blue, clear and wide—but filled with a shock and a panic that stopped him short.

She stared at him blankly and he held out his hands in a show of innocence. 'I'm Nic,' he said, realising she had no idea who he was. 'Dominic—Kate's brother. She said to drop by and pick up my keys?'

'Oh, God,' she said. 'I'd completely forgotten.'

But still she didn't move. Her eyes did, though, dropping to his vest and running shorts, moving as far down as his ankles before her eyes met his again. There was interest there, he could see, even behind her confusion and distress.

'Is everything all right?' he asked again, though everything about her—her posture, her expression—told him that it wasn't.

'Oh, fine,' she said.

He could see the effort it took to pull the muscles of her face into a brave smile, but it wasn't enough to cover the undercurrents of worry that lay beneath. There was something about that contrast that made him curious—more than curious—to know the layers of this woman.

'*My* sister...' she said, boldly attempting nonchalance. 'She never gives me much notice when she needs a babysitter.'

Which was about five per cent of the truth, if he had to guess. He found himself looking deep into her eyes, trying to see her truths, all the things that she wasn't saying. Was there some sort of trick here? Was this something Kate had set up? Surely she'd never be so cruel, never willingly expose him to so much pain?

But he wanted to know more about this woman, he acknowledged. Wanted to untangle her mysteries.

Then he could ignore the screams of the baby no longer, and knew that he mustn't even think it. He should turn and walk away from her and the little bundle of trouble now. Before he got drawn in, before wounds that had taken a decade to become numb were reopened.

But he couldn't, *wouldn't* walk away from someone so obviously in trouble. Couldn't abandon a child, however much it might hurt him. He'd discovered that on his first trip to India, when he'd seen children used as slave labour, making clothes to be sold on British high streets. He'd not been able to leave without doing *something*, without working to improve the shattered lives that he'd witnessed.

Now, ten years later, the charity he'd founded had helped hundreds, thousands of children from exploitation or worse. But that didn't make him any more able to ignore this single child's cries.

Distressed children needed help—whoever they were, wherever they were living. He finally forced himself to look at the crying baby—and felt the bottom fall out of all his worries. He was in serious trouble, and any thoughts of walking away became an impossibility. That was a newborn baby…as in hours-old new. Completely helpless, completely vulnerable and—by the look on Lily's face—a complete surprise.

The baby's crying picked up another notch and Lily bounced it optimistically. But, if he had to guess, she didn't have what that baby needed.

'Did your sister leave some milk? Or some formula?'

She looked up and held his gaze, her eyes still a complicated screen of half-truths. There was something dangerously attractive in that expression, something drawing him in against his better judgement. There was a bond growing between himself and Lily— he could feel it. And some connection with this baby's story was at the heart of it. It was dangerous, and he wanted nothing to do with it, but still he didn't walk away.

'She asked me to pick some up,' she replied, obviously thinking on her feet. 'Thanks for stopping, but I have to get to the shop.'

He chose his next words carefully, knowing that he mustn't scare her off, but seeing by the shocked look on her face that she hadn't quite grasped yet the trouble that this newborn baby might be in. Who left an hours-old baby with a relative who clearly wasn't expecting her? There was more, much more, to this story, and he suspected that there were layers of complications that neither of them yet understood.

'That's quite a noise she's making. How about to be on the safe side we get her checked by a doctor? I saw that the hospital round the corner has a walk-in clinic.'

At that, Lily physically shook herself, pulled her shoulders back and grabbed the baby a little tighter. There was something about seeing the obvious concern and turmoil in her expression that made him want to wrap his arms around her and promise her that everything would be okay. But he was the last person on earth who could promise her that, who could even believe that it might be true.

'Maybe you're right,' she said, walking away from the open front door and through the garden gate.

'Kate's keys are in the top drawer in the hall. Can you pull the door closed on your way out?'

And then she was speed-walking down the street, the baby still clutched tightly to her, still wailing. He glanced at the house and hesitated. He needed his keys, but he could hardly leave Lily's house with the door wide open—the woman hadn't even picked up her handbag. Did she have her own keys? Her wallet? So he had no choice but to grab her bag and his keys and jog in the direction of those newborn wails.

He just wanted to be sure that the baby was going to be okay, he told himself.

'I'll walk with you,' he said as he caught Lily up.

The words were out of his mouth before he had a chance to stop them. However much he might wish he hadn't stumbled on this little family drama, he had. He might be wrong, but gut instinct and not a little cir-cumstantial evidence told him that this child had just been abandoned—which meant, of course, that both mother and baby could be in danger.

He tried to focus on practicalities, tried to put thoughts of what might have been had he and Lily met on any other sunny day out of his mind. He should call Kate. And maybe the police—they were the best people to ensure that the baby's mother was safe and well. But he couldn't ignore the fascination that he felt about Lily. There was an energy that seemed to pull him towards her and push him away at the same time—it had him curious, had him interested.

CHAPTER TWO

LILY EYED NIC, where he leaned against the wall by the door—a position he'd adopted almost as soon as they'd been shown into this room. He looked at the door often, as if reminding himself that it was there. That he could use it any time. So why was he still here?

Under normal circumstances she'd say that an attractive man, background-checked by her BFF, somewhat scantily clad, could involve himself in her life at any time he chose—as long as she had the option of checking out those long, lean thighs. But he really had killer timing.

She didn't have time to ogle; she didn't have time for his prying questions. All she could think about was her sister, Helen, and the baby, and what she needed to do to take care of both of them.

She paced the room, glancing over at the baby and wondering what on earth they were doing to her. Had they found something wrong? If everything was okay, surely someone would have told her by now. She hadn't wanted to hand her over to the doctors, but she'd had no choice.

It was becoming a pattern, this letting go, this watching from afar. She'd lost her father before she

was born, to nothing more dramatic than disinterest
and a lost phone number. Her mother had died the year
that Lily had turned thirteen, and it seemed her sister
had been drifting further and further from her since
that day. All she wanted was a family to take care of,
to take care of her, and yet that seemed too much to
ask from the universe.

And now someone had called the police, and her sister was going to be in more trouble than ever, pushed
further from her. She tried not to think of the alterna-
tive. Of Helen out there needing help and not getting
it. If it took the authorities getting involved to get her
safe and well, then Lily was all for it.

She started pacing again, craning her neck each
time she passed the baby to try and get a glimpse of
what was happening.

'Just a couple of tests,' the doctor had said. How
could that possibly take this long?

She glanced across at Nic, and then quickly away.
How had she never met Kate's brother before? Surely
there should be some sort of declaration when you became best friends with someone about any seriously
attractive siblings. He'd been abroad, she remembered
Kate saying. He ran a charity that tried to improve conditions for child workers in factories in the developing
world. He'd recently been headhunted by one of the
big retailers that he'd campaigned against, and would
be sitting on their board, in charge of cleaning up their
supply chain. So attractive, humanitarian, and with a
job in retail. There should definitely be a disclaimer for
this sort of thing.

But there was something about him that made her
nervous—some tension in his body and his voice

that told her this man had secrets too: secrets that she couldn't understand. It was telling her to stay away. That he was off-limits. A warning she didn't need.

Nic came to stand beside her. 'Try not to worry. I'm sure that everything is fine—they're just being thorough.'

Lily bit her lip and nodded. She knew that he was right. He gestured her back to a seat and cleared his throat, giving her a rare direct look.

She continued pacing the room, waiting for news— until she heard a shriek, and then she was by the bed, her arms out, already reaching for the baby.

The doctor barely looked up from where he was pricking the little one's heel with a needle.

'I'm sorry, we're not quite done.'

'You're hurting her!'

Lily scooped the baby into her arms as she wiped away the spot of blood from her foot and cooed soothing noises, gently rocking her. Back in Lily's embrace, the baby stopped crying and nuzzled closer. Lily leaned over, instinctively shielding the baby from the doctor who had hurt her, until she felt the little body relax. She kissed the baby's forehead, leaving her own face close for a moment, breathing in her baby smell. Once she was satisfied that she was calmed she looked up at the doctor, and instantly stiffened her resolve at the look of disapproval on his face.

'I'm her aunt,' she stated, as if that were explanation enough for everything. 'Have you finished with the tests? It looks as if she's had enough for now.'

She stared him down until he conceded that they had everything they needed. That was when she spotted Nic, looking grey and decidedly ill by the door.

'When she cried out…' he said. 'I thought…'

Whatever he had thought had scared him witless, she realised, instinctively taking a step towards him.

'She's fine. We're fine,' she told him, in the same soothing tone she'd used with the baby. She turned her towards him. 'Look, she's settled now.'

He breathed a sigh of relief and Lily could almost see the adrenaline leaching from his body, leaving him limp and drawn. She met his eyes, looking for answers there, but instead saw only pain. An old pain, she guessed, one that had been lived with a long time and had become so familiar it was hardly noticed. Until something happened—a baby screamed—and it felt like new again.

For a moment she wished that she could soothe him as easily as she had the baby—smooth those creases from his face and the pain from his body. But something told her that taking this man in her arms would bring him anything but peace. She pressed herself back against the wall, trying to put whatever space she could between them.

'Is everything okay?' she asked.

'Fine.'

Nic's reply was terse, sharper than she'd expected, and she saw the fear and hurt in his expression being carefully shut down, stowed away.

'I need to grab a cup of coffee. Do you want to find the canteen? We've been here for hours.'

And leave the baby alone with strangers? 'I'm fine, thanks. I don't want to leave her.'

He gave her a shrewd look. 'I'll go, then,' he said, pushing himself away from the wall.

He looked better now, as he had in her front garden, all bronzed skin and taut muscles. No sign now of the man who had looked as if he might slide down the wall from fear.

When he returned with coffee and cake his manner was brisk and his eyes guarded. *Good*å, Lily thought. *Guarded is good. If we're both being careful, both backing away slowly from whatever this energy between us is, then we're safe.*

'I've got to go,' he said. 'I promised that I'd meet Kate and she's not answering her phone so I can't cancel. I don't want to leave her stranded.'

And then he was off—out of their lives, and no doubt relieved to be so. She held in her heavy sigh until he'd slipped out of the door with her polite words of thanks.

CHAPTER THREE

KATE BURST THROUGH the door of the treatment room, wearing her air of drama queen as if it was this season's must-have.

Lily smiled at the arrival of her best friend. If anyone was going to help her make sense of this situation it would be Kate, with her remarkable ability to see through half-truths and get straight to the point.

'So I get back from court and pop in to see my brother in his new flat, and he's got this crazy story about your dear sister and a baby and a hospital. I didn't have a clue what was going on, so I thought I'd better get down here and find out just what he's talking about. Explain, Lily! Where's this flippin' baby come from? What are you doing here? And why does my brother look so cagey whenever I mention your name?'

Lily couldn't help but laugh—trust Kate to boil this down to the bare essentials.

'She's Helen's baby. Helen left her on my doorstep with a note. Your brother was passing by to pick up his keys and...and kept us company while we were waiting here.'

It was rare that she saw Kate lost for words, but she dropped into a chair now, silent, and Lily could practically see the thoughts being processed behind her eyes. Her barrister's brain was reading all the evidence, everything that Lily was saying, and everything she wasn't.

'Okay, give it to me again. And this time with details.'

Lily sighed and took a breath, wondering how many times she would have to repeat everything that had happened. But when she came to talking about Nic her words stumbled and faltered.

'Nic turned up to collect his keys just as I'd been left literally holding the baby and was freaking out. He suggested we walk over here and have her checked out.'

'And then he waited with you? How long for?'

Lily glanced at her watch. 'A couple of hours, I guess.'

Kate blew out a deliberate breath, and Lily raised her eyebrows.

'What?'

'Nothing…nothing,' Kate said, but Lily had known her long enough to know that she was hiding something.

'Not nothing,' she told her best friend. 'Definitely *something.*'

Kate looked at her for a long time before she replied.

'Something,' she agreed, nodding, her eyes sad. 'But not my something to tell. Can we leave it at that?'

Lily nodded. Though she was intrigued, her friend's rare sombre tone had pulled her up short and warned her to stop digging.

'So you and my brother, then…?'

'It's not like that.' The denial came to Lily's lips as soon as she realised what Kate was getting at. 'I don't think he wanted to be here at all. He looked like he was going to bolt the whole time.'

'So why didn't he?'

True to form, Kate had hit on the one question that Lily had been searching for an answer to—to no avail.

'I've no idea.'

'I've got one or two,' Kate said with a sly grin. 'So what happens with the baby now?'

Another question Lily had no answer to.

No doubt between the hospital staff and the police someone would be arranging for a social worker to visit her. But she had no intention of letting her niece be looked after by anyone but herself. She knew that she could look after her—she already ran a business from home, and had flexibility in her hours and her work. It was one of the things that she enjoyed most about her job as a freelance web designer—the chance to balance work and home life. She'd manage her work commitments around caring for the baby—whatever it took to keep the little girl safe and with her family.

'She's coming home with me.'

Lily gulped at the baldness of that statement, and backtracked.

'Until we can find Helen.'

'Right. And then you're going to hand her over to a woman who's been living God-knows-where and doing God-knows-what for years?'

'Helen's her mother—'

'And she seems pretty clear about who she wants taking care of her daughter. I'm not saying that taking her home is a bad thing—she's family. Of course you want to look after her. I'm just saying it looks like it might be slightly more commitment than a regular babysitting gig. Are you ready for that?'

Ready for a family? It was what she'd wanted for as long as she could remember. She'd been lucky after her mother had died. She'd been placed with a wonderful foster family who had slowly and gently helped her to come to terms with her grief. She'd certainly been luckier than her sister, who, at sixteen, had decided that she was old enough to look after herself.

They'd exchanged letters and emails, but over the years they'd become less and less frequent, until now she couldn't even rely on a card at Christmas. All she wanted was a family of her own. To recapture something of what the three of them—herself, her mum and Helen—had had before the accident.

She'd even looked into ways to build that family. After her own experience of foster care she'd thought of offering her house to children who might need it.

The old family home had seemed echoey and empty when she'd moved back in when she was eighteen. Her mother's will had protected it in a trust for her and her sister, but it had been lonely with no one to share it with. But she'd never considered she'd ever be handed a newborn baby and asked if she was ready to be a parent.

'We have to find Helen,' Lily said. 'That's as far as I can think right now.'

'There is one slight flaw in that plan,' Kate said.

'Only one?' Lily asked, only half joking.

'Your house. It's currently a building site, and— unless I'm much mistaken—not exactly ready for a newborn…whether she's going to be there permanently or not.'

Lily's face fell. In all the drama she'd somehow managed to forget the chaotic state of her house. There was no way that she could take a baby back there. And if she couldn't take care of her niece that left only one option. Letting social services place her with strangers. Her gut recoiled at the thought of losing another member of her family, of her and Helen and their past being fractured even further.

'Don't look like that,' Kate said. 'This is not insurmountable. We can sort this out—'

'That's really kind,' Lily said, her mind still racing, 'but your place barely has enough room for me to pull out the sofa bed. I'm not sure that—'

'Not *me*!' Kate exclaimed. 'Good God, no. We'd lose the baby under a stack of briefs or something. Nic's place—it's perfect.'

Lily gave a little choke.

'Nic's place? I couldn't possibly impose…'

She couldn't share a flat with that man—not when she felt drawn to him and afraid of that attraction in equal measure. When her skin tingled just from being in the same room as him.

'Honestly, you should see his place. It's ridiculous. A penthouse—overlooking the river, naturally. He told me it was something to do with investing his golden handshake money, and London property prices, and being able to do so much more with the money once he sold up. Personally, I think it might have something to do with sleeping in hostels for the best part of a decade. It's huge, and he's barely ever there.'

Even the thought of a Thameside penthouse couldn't convince her that spending more time with a man who had her wanting him and wanting to run from him was a good idea. But what choice did she have? If she wanted to take care of her niece she couldn't afford to be picky about what help she accepted. And, anyway, what she thought was probably irrelevant…

'Nic would never—'

'Nic will be travelling on and off for the next few months. He's due to fly out again tomorrow, I think. You won't see each other much. And if the man who's preached charity and child welfare at me for the past ten years can't see it in his heart to give an abandoned baby a home for a few months, then I'll disown him.'

Somehow Lily didn't think that was a threat that would carry much weight for Nic.

'*And* trash his lovely new apartment,' she added.

'Okay, ask him,' Lily said eventually. What choice did she have?

An awkward silence fell for a few moments, until Kate obviously couldn't stand the quiet any longer.

'So, does this little one have a name, or what?'

Lily shook her head. 'Helen didn't exactly say.'

'Well, that's just not right, is it? She's had a rough enough start in life already, without ending up being named just Baby Girl. So what are we going to go for: naming her after a pop star or a soap star. Or we could go big and Hollywood?'

Lily raised an eyebrow.

'Okay, so I'm guessing that's a no. What do *you* suggest?'

Lily looked closely at the baby, trying to work out who she was. 'Look at her,' Lily said. 'All pretty and pink and fresh and soft…like a flower. A rose. What about Rosie?'

'I think it's perfect,' Kate agreed. 'Little Rosie—welcome to the world.'

Nic's feet pounded on the pavement as he tried to get thoughts of Lily Baker out of his head—with zero success. Since the moment he'd met her she'd invaded all of his thoughts, forcing him to keep busy, keep working, keep running. But even two days on his body still wouldn't co-operate, refusing to find the quiet place in his mind where he could retreat from the world.

His sister wasn't exactly helping, with her pointed remarks and regular updates on how baby and aunt were faring. Did she think he couldn't see what she was doing? That the strings of her puppeteering were somehow invisible? But he *did* wonder how the baby was. Kate had said that she was doing well, and the doctors hadn't seemed worried when he'd left the hospital, but he knew better than most how precarious a new life was, how quickly it might be lost.

Turning for home, he tried to find his usual rhythm, but his feet carried him faster than he wanted, rushing him.

His mobile rang as he reached his flat, and Kate's latest unsubtle update gave him all he needed to know. No news on the missing sister. Baby apparently doing well in hospital. But somehow it wasn't enough. What did that mean anyway? 'Doing well in hospital.' Surely if the baby was 'doing well' then she wouldn't be in hospital at all. She'd be home, tucked into a cot, safe. And this time Kate had not said anything about Lily.

He hadn't been able to think of a way to ask about

her without raising suspicious eyebrows. He could hardly say, *And how about the aunt? The one with the glowing skin and the complicated expressions and the fierce independence? How's she getting on?*

But he was desperate to know. Lily Baker seemed to have soaked into his mind until his every thought was coloured by her. It was no good. The only way he was going to get this woman and her niece out of his mind was to get some answers, some closure.

He saw her as soon as he walked onto the ward. He should have known that she would have been there all night. Had been there for two nights, he guessed. Her hair was mussed, rubbing up against the side of the chair she'd curled into, but her face was relaxed, looking so different from when she'd worn that troubled, burdened expression before.

He knocked on the door, aware that he didn't want to answer the questions that being caught watching her sleep would give rise to. Lily sat bolt upright at the sound, her hand instinctively reaching for the cot, eyes flying towards the baby. Only once she was satisfied that she was sleeping soundly did she turn towards the door. Her eyes widened in surprise, and he realised how unguarded she was in the moment after waking—how her expression shifted as her eyes skimmed over him appreciatively.

There was no mistaking the interest there, and his stomach tightened in response as he fought down his instinctive reaction. Eventually her eyes reached his, and he saw her barriers start to build as she emerged properly from sleep. Her back straightened and her face grew composed.

The rational, sensible, *thinking* part of his brain

breathed a sigh of relief. He was glad that she was as wary as he was of this energy he felt flowing and sparking between them, the pull that he felt between their bodies. Much as he might find her attractive, he would never act on that. He wasn't the kind of man she needed in her life. When she found someone she'd need a partner—a father for this child and the ones that would come in the future. She would need someone she could rely on, and he knew that he wasn't capable of being that man.

But the part of his brain less removed from his primal ancestors groaned, trying to persuade him to get that dreamy look back on her face, to seduce her into softness.

'Morning,' he said, rather more briskly than he'd intended. 'I brought coffee. I know the stuff here's awful.'

'Morning. Thanks…'

Her voice was as wary as her expression, and he guessed that he wasn't the only one who'd thought that they would never see each other again after he'd left the hospital. He wondered if she'd found it as impossible not to think of him as he had of her. Of course not, he reasoned. She had the baby to think about—there was probably no room in her life right now for anything other than feeding, nappies and sleep.

At the sound of her voice the baby had started to stir, and Lily automatically reached out a hand to stroke her cheek.

'How is she?'

'She's fine…good. They've said that I can take her home today.'

Home. So that settled it, then. Kate had been right

the other day—Lily was going to look after the baby as her sister had asked. And that meant he'd been right to fight off this attraction. Because if there was one thing he was certain of it was that he could never get involved with someone who had a child. He could never again open himself up to that sort of hurt.

Even if Lily's sister returned, he couldn't imagine that Lily saw a future without children. He'd seen the melting look in her eye as she'd gazed down at her niece—there was no hiding her maternal instincts.

'That's good. I'm glad she's okay.' Now that he had his answer he felt awkward, not sure why he had come. No doubt Lily was wondering what he was doing there, too. Or perhaps not. Perhaps his real interest was as transparent to her as it had been opaque to him.

Perhaps he had imagined this energy and attraction—imagined the way her eyes widened whenever her skin brushed against his, the way she flushed in those rare moments when they both risked eye contact. Maybe she saw him as nothing other than the Good Samaritan who had happened to be there when she'd needed someone. If only she knew that when someone else had really needed him, when they'd relied on him to be there for them, he'd let them down.

He glanced up at the name plate above the crib and realised that the little girl was no longer Baby Baker.

'Rosie?' he asked, surprise in his voice. Kate hadn't mentioned that.

'It seemed to suit her,' Lily said with a shrug. 'It's not official yet. If Helen doesn't like it…'

'It's pretty.'

'Look, I hate to ask this when you're already doing so much for us…'

Lily glanced at the door and Nic guessed what was coming. Instantly he wished himself anywhere in the world but here. But Lily was still speaking, and he knew that it was too late.

'…just for fifteen minutes or so, while I grab a shower. I know the nurses are listening out for her, but I hate the thought of her being alone. I know I can trust you with her.'

A lump blocked his throat and he couldn't force the word *no* out past it. He'd not been responsible for a child since the morning he'd found his son, cold and still in his crib. But the look on Lily's face—the trust that he saw there—touched his heart in a way he hadn't realised was even still possible. And more than anything he wanted to know that the baby—little Rosie—was going to be okay. That was why he'd dragged himself down here, after all. Fifteen minutes alone with a sleeping baby—surely he could manage that, could ensure that she was safe while Lily was away?

He nodded. 'Sure, go ahead. You look like you could do with a break.'

Her smile held for a moment before her face fell. Oh, God, that wasn't what he'd meant at all. He'd all but said, *You look awful,* hadn't he? What was it about this woman that made it so impossible for him to function anything like normal?

He started back-pedalling fast. 'Sorry, I didn't mean it like that at all. You look fine. I mean—I just meant you've slept in that chair two nights in a row, and I bet you're tired. You look great.'

This wasn't getting any better. But Lily grinned at him, probably enjoying his discomfort, and the fact that he didn't seem at all able to remove his foot from his mouth.

A disconcerting noise and a very bad smell halted Nic's apology in its tracks, and as he caught Lily's eyes they both laughed.

'Well, perhaps if you change her I might find it in my heart to forgive you.'

Before he had a chance to argue she was out of the room, leaving him alone with the baby. This was not at all what he'd expected when he'd reluctantly agreed to watch a sleeping baby for fifteen minutes, but he reached for the nappies and the cotton wool, acting on instinct.

He narrowed his eyes, trying not to see Rosie's little pink cheeks or her tiny fingers. He just had to concentrate on the task in hand, and he could do that without really looking at her, without thinking about the fact that this little body was a whole new life—maybe a hundred years of potential all contained in seven pounds of toes and belly and new baby smell. Without thinking about his son.

He had nearly finished the nappy when Rosie began to fuss. As he fastened the poppers on her Babygro and washed his hands, he silently pleaded with her not to start crying. But her face screwed up and the tears started, and her banshee-like wail was impossible to ignore. He shut his eyes as he scooped a hand under her head and another under her bottom and lifted her to his shoulder, making soothing noises that he hoped would quiet her. He tried not to think at all as he bounced her gently, waiting for her tears to stop, tried not to think of the first time he had held his son, Max.

Or the last time.

The memory made him clutch Rosie a little tighter, hold her a little safer, knowing how precarious a young life could be. Eventually her cries slowed to sniffles as she snuggled closer to his shoulder and started looking for a source of food. He looked around the room, wondering where he'd lay his hands on formula and a bottle. He could ask the nurses, he supposed.

He transferred Rosie to the crook of one arm, only flinching momentarily at the remembered familiarity of the movement, and headed for the door. As it opened he was greeted by the sight of Lily, fresh from the shower, with no make-up and her hair pulled back, and it took his breath away.

Any chance of kidding himself that his interest was only in Rosie's welfare was lost. It was more than that. It was...*her*. He just couldn't stop thinking about her. But that was the problem. If he'd met Lily just one day earlier, before her sister had turned up with a baby, he wouldn't have hesitated to explore this connection between them, to imagine Lily looking as she did now— all fresh and pink and polished from the shower. But the shower would have been in his flat, and she'd have just left his bed.

Everything about her fascinated him. But she'd taken in her sister's child without a thought. And because of that he knew that they could never be happy together. He could see from her every look at Rosie that Lily was born to be a mother. She wanted a family, and he could never give her that—nor could he ask her to sacrifice it for him. There was no point considering a brief fling, either: a taste of her would never be enough—and if he started to fall for her then how would he make himself stop? And all that was even without the added complication of his sister's unspoken threats to hurt him in a *very* sensitive place if he messed with her best friend.

'I was just going to try and find her a bottle.'

Lily waved the bottle of formula she was carrying. 'No need. I see you couldn't resist a cuddle? I don't blame you—she's very squeezable.'

'It's not like that,' he replied instinctively. 'She was crying, that's all. Here—take her.' He almost shoved the baby at her, alarmed at how quickly he'd adapted, how natural it had felt to hold her.

'What's wrong?' Lily asked, her eyes wary. 'I don't mind you holding her.'

'I know.' Nic breathed slowly, trying to fight the urge to run from the room, knowing that he should explain his harsh words to Lily. Hating the wary, guarded look that had just entered her eyes. 'I'm just not good around babies.'

She glanced down at Rosie, who looked happy and content. 'Seems like you're pretty good to me.'

An awkward silence fell between them, and Lily looked as if she was trying to find the right words to say something. Suddenly he wanted out of the room. Her face was serious, and he wondered if she had guessed about his past, or if Kate had told her about it. His heart started racing as he remembered all the times he had failed at that in the past. All the broken conversations, the broken relationships that had followed.

'Nic, I don't know how to thank you for being there for us the other day. And Kate told me—'

Before he knew it he was reaching for her, wanting to stem the flow of her words. He didn't want to know what Kate had told her of his failings as a father and a partner.

He'd do anything to stop her speaking.

His lips pressed against hers as his fingers cradled her jaw, and for just a second he wondered what would happen if she opened her mouth to him, if her body softened and relaxed against him. If this kiss changed from a desperate plea for mercy to something softer, something more passionate. But he pulled away before it had the chance.

'I'm sorry,' he said, shutting his eyes against the confusion on her face and heading towards the door. 'I shouldn't have done that.'

Lily stood shell-shocked in the middle of the hospital room, the baby in one arm and the bottle held loosely in her other hand. What on earth had just happened? She'd been about to thank him for letting them stay with him—just until the work on her house was finished. But the cornered look in his eyes had stopped her words, and the kiss he'd pressed against her lips had stopped her thoughts.

It had been difficult enough to see herself living in his apartment. How was she meant to do it now, with this kiss between them, dragging up every fantasy she'd been forcing herself to bury? If she'd had any other option she'd have jumped at it. But Kate had been right. This was her only choice—kiss or no kiss.

She wondered at the expression on Nic's face, at the way he had cradled Rosie in one arm as if it was the most natural thing in the world. He'd obviously been around babies before. Had he been a father once? Was that what was behind the fear and the pain she saw in him? She couldn't imagine that anything but the loss of a child could draw such a picture of grief on some-one's face. He carried a pain that was still raw and devastating—so why on earth had he agreed to let her live with him?

She spun at the sound of a knock to the door, won-dering for an instant if it was Nic, back to rescind his invitation, to tell her she wasn't welcome anywhere near him. But instead of Nic it was her social worker standing in the doorway, case file in hand and a smile on her face.

CHAPTER FOUR

LILY LEANT AGAINST the wall of the lift as it climbed to the top of the building and snuck another look at Rosie, sleeping in her pram, not quite believing that she was really going to do this. But Kate had promised her that Nic was okay with it. He would be away on a business trip for the next week at least, so she'd have plenty of time to settle in and find her feet before she had to think about him. Or that kiss.

What had he been thinking? Perhaps the same as her—nothing. Perhaps the touch of their lips had banished all rational thought and left him as confused as she was.

At least all the paperwork and everything in officialdom was ticking along nicely. It was just a case of getting the right legal papers in order, and making sure that Helen had the medical help—both physical and mental—that she needed to get and stay well. There had been no talk of prosecution for abandonment—only concern for Helen and Rosie's welfare.

A stack of half-opened parcels littered the hallway, making the apartment look less bachelor sophisticated and more like a second hand sale. Kate must have beaten her here and picked up all the internet shopping that Lily had done while she was in the hospital with Rosie. They had some work ahead of them to get the apartment baby-ready—that was clear.

She peeked into the living room and was tempted to shiver at the abundance of black leather, smoked glass and chrome. Everything in the room shone, and Lily wondered if Nic was quite mad for letting them stay here. One thing was for sure: even with Rosie on her best behaviour it wasn't going to be easy keeping the place looking this show-home perfect.

'Kate?' Lily called out as she stood in the living room with Rosie in her arms, her eyes drawn to the glass walls with a view out over the river. 'Are you here?'

A voice sounded from the end of the hallway.

'In here!' she shouted. 'I'm just doing battle with the cot.'

Lily followed the sound of Kate's swearing and found herself in a luxurious bedroom. Between the doorway and the enormous pillow-topped bed Kate's curly head was just visible between the bars of a half-built cot.

'Are you winning?' Lily asked with a laugh.

'Depends on who's keeping score,' came the reply, along with another string of expletives.

Lily covered Rosie's ears and tutted.

'Sorry, Rosie,' Kate said, finally dropping the screwdriver and climbing out from the pile of flat-packed pieces. 'How are we doing?' she asked as she crossed the room to give Rosie a squeeze and Lily a kiss on the cheek.

'She's fine,' Lily told her. 'Clean bill of health. Thanks so much for getting started with this.' She waved a hand towards the cot.

'Don't be daft. It's nothing. Now, are you going to put the baby down and give me a hand?'

'Let me just grab her carrycot and I'll see if she'll go down.'

As Lily walked back into the hallway she jumped against the wall at the sight of a man's dark shadow up ahead of her.

'Nic…?' she said, holding Rosie a little tighter to her.

As Nic took a step forward his face came into the light and she could see the shock and surprise written across his features.

'Lily, what the hell—?'

'Kate!'

She wasn't sure which of them shouted first, but as it became apparent that Nic had had no idea she was going to be there Lily felt flames of embarrassment lick up her cheeks, colouring her skin. Oh, Kate had some explaining to do.

Kate at least had the good grace to look sheepish when she emerged into the hallway.

'What the hell is *she* doing here?'

Lily's gaze snapped back to Nic at the anger in his voice and she felt herself physically recoil. She was as surprised to see him there as he was to find them both in the flat—Kate had promised her he would be out of town for at least a week yet—but the venom in his voice was unexpected and more than a little offensive.

'Nic!' Kate admonished. 'Don't talk about Lily like that. I promise you, I can explain. You're not meant to *be* here.'

'It's my home, Kate. Where else would I be?'

'Well, India, for a start. And then Bangladesh. And Rome. And...'

'And I decided to spend a few weeks in the office before I go abroad again. I pushed some of my trips back. Not that I need to explain myself—*I'm* not the one who's in the wrong here.'

He threw a look at Lily that was impossible to misinterpret.

'Look...' Kate was using her best lawyer voice, and Lily suddenly felt a pang of sympathy for Nic. When she took that tone there was little doubt that she was going to get her own way.

But it didn't matter how Kate was planning on sweet-talking her way out of 'stretching the truth', as she was bound to call it. There was no way she could stay here—not with the looks of pure anger that Nic was sending their way.

'This is how I see things: Lily needs somewhere to stay. Rosie can't go back to Lily's as it has no kitchen, no back wall, isn't warm or even watertight. You have a big, ridiculous apartment that was *meant* to be empty for at least the next week, and which even when you're here has more available square footage than most detached family homes.'

Nic opened his mouth to argue, but Kate held up a hand, cutting him off.

'You, Mr Humanitarian, having spent the last decade saving the world one child factory worker at a time, have the opportunity to practise what you preach here. Charity begins at home, you know.'

Lily rolled her eyes at the cliché, and from the corner of her eye caught just the hint of a smirk starting at the corner of Nic's lips. When she built up the courage to look at him straight she saw that the tension had dropped from his face and he was smiling openly at his sister.

'Oh, you're good,' he said. '*Very* good. I hope they're paying you well.'

'And I'm worth every penny,' she confirmed. 'Now, seeing as you're home, I don't want to step on any toes.' She thrust the screwdriver into his hand and Nic had no choice but to take it. 'I'll leave you two to work out the details.'

And before Lily could pick up her jaw from the floor Kate had disappeared out of the front door, leaving her holding the baby and Nic staring at the screwdriver.

'I'm *so* sorry,' she said, rushing to put Rosie down in her pram and take the screwdriver from Nic's hand. 'She told me that you'd okayed it, but I should have guessed…I'll pack our stuff up and order a cab and we'll be out of your hair.'

Nic gave her a long look, and she watched, fascinated, as emotions chased over his face, first creasing his forehead and his eyes, then smoothing across his cheeks with something like resignation.

'Where will you go?'

'Oh…' Lily flapped a hand, hoping that the distraction would cover the fact that she didn't have a clue what her next move was. 'Back to mine, of course. It's not that bad. I'm sure I can come up with another plan.'

Nic rubbed his hand across his forehead.

'What plan?'

'A hotel,' Lily said, improvising wildly. 'Maybe a temporary rental.'

He let out a long sigh and shook his head slowly.

'Stay here.'

'Nic, I couldn't—'

Lily started to speak, but Nic's raised hand stopped her.

'Kate's right. You need a place to stay. I have loads of room here.'

A warm flood of relief passed through Lily. For a moment she'd thought that she might be out on the streets—worse, that she wouldn't be able to provide Rosie with the home she so desperately needed. And it was the thought that Rosie needed somewhere safe to stay that had her swallowing her pride and nodding to agree with what was almost certainly a terrible idea.

'Thank you. I promise we'll keep out of your way.'

Lily stood in the kitchen, coffee cup in hand, surveying the vast array of knobs and buttons on the espresso machine built into the kitchen wall. She'd already boiled the kettle, intimidated by the levers and chrome of the machine, but in the absence of a jar of good old instant coffee she was going to have to do battle with this beast. She tried the sleek-looking knob on the left— and jumped back from the torrent of steam that leapt from the nozzle hidden beneath. Thank God she'd left Rosie safely sleeping in their room.

A lightly haired forearm appeared over her shoulder and turned off the knob, shutting down the steam and leaving her red-faced and perspiring.

'Here,' Nic said, taking the cup from her hand. 'Let me.'

'Thanks.' Lily handed over coffee responsibility gratefully, and leaned back against the kitchen counter.

Embarrassment sat in the air between them, and Lily's mind couldn't help but fly back to that kiss in the hospital. The way that Nic's lips had pressed so firmly against hers, as if he was fighting himself even as he was kissing her. He'd known that it was a bad idea at the time—she was sure of that. And yet he'd done it anyway. Now they were living together—and apparently they were just going to ignore that it had happened. But even with them saying nothing, it was there, in the atmosphere between them, making them awkward with each other.

She wondered whether she should say something, try and clear the air, but then she heard a cry from the bedroom.

'You go and get Rosie. I'll sort the coffee.'

Was that an invitation? Were they going to sit down and drink a cup of coffee like civilised adults? And if they did would he bring up the kiss? Would she? Surely they couldn't just carry on as if nothing had happened. It was making her clumsy around him, and she could never feel relaxed or at home unless they both loosened up. Maybe that was what he was hoping for. That he'd be able to make things awkward enough that she'd have no choice but to leave. Then he'd get his apartment back without having to be the big bad wolf in the story.

Lily had returned to the kitchen with the baby in one arm, and set about making up a bottle for her. Nic watched them carefully, knowing that a gentleman would offer to help, but finding himself not quite able to live up to that ideal.

'It's good we've got a chance to sit down and talk,' he said as he carried their coffees over to the kitchen island. 'I wanted to apologise for the other day. The…

the kiss. And the way I left things. I know I was a bit abrupt.'

'It's fine—' Lily started, but he held up a hand to stop her.

The memory of the confusion on her face had been haunting him, and he knew that if they were to live together, even if it was only temporarily, he had to make sure she knew exactly why that kiss had been such a mistake. Why she shouldn't hope for or expect another.

They had only known each other for a few days, but after that parting shot at the hospital he wouldn't be able to blame her if she'd misinterpreted things—if she'd read more into that kiss than he'd ever wanted to give. She deserved better than that…better than a man with his limitations. And with Rosie in her life she was going to have to demand more. Demand someone who would support her family life whatever happened. He'd already been tested on that front and found wanting. It was only fair that Lily knew where they both stood.

'Please,' he continued, 'I want to explain.'

A line appeared between her brows, as if she had suddenly realised that this was a conversation neither of them would enjoy. The suggestion that she was hurt pained him physically, but he forced himself to continue—for both their sakes.

'There's no need to explain anything, but I'll listen if you want me to.'

She glanced over at the counter, her edginess showing in the way she was fidgeting with her coffee cup. The anxious expression on her face told him so much. She'd guessed something of his history. Guessed, at least, how hard it was for him to be around Rosie. Had she seen how impossible it would be for them even to be friends?

Not that *friends* would ever have really worked, he mused, when the sight of her running a hand through her hair made him desperate to reach across and see if it felt as silky as it looked. When he'd lain awake every night since they'd last met remembering the feel of her lips under his, imagining the softness of her skin and the suppleness of her body.

He kept his eyes on Lily, never dropping them to the little girl in her arms, not risking the pain that would assault him if he even glanced at Rosie or acknowledged that she was there. The way Lily looked at him, her clear blue gaze, gave him no room to lie or evade. He knew that faced with that open, honest look he'd be able to speak nothing but the truth.

'There's something I need to tell you…' he started.

His voice held the hint of a croak, and he felt the cold climbing his chest, wondered how on earth he was meant to get these words out. How he was meant to relive the darkest days of his life with this woman who a week ago had been a stranger.

'I know there's something between us—at least I know that I've started to feel something for you. But I need you to know that I won't act again on what I feel.'

He kept his voice deliberately flat, forcing the emotion from it as he'd had to do when faced with people living and working in inhuman conditions. And he looked down at the table, unable to bear her sympathetic scrutiny. Or what if he had read this wrong— what if there was nothing between them at all? What if he'd imagined the chemistry that kept drawing them together even as it hurt him? It wasn't as if he'd even given her a chance to return his kiss. He risked a glance up at her. Her lip was caught between her teeth and the line had reappeared on her forehead. But he wasn't sure what he was seeing on her face. Not clear disappointment. Definitely not surprise.

'It's fine, Nic. You don't need to say any more.'

'I do.'

He wanted her to know, wanted to acknowledge his feelings even if just this once. Wanted her to understand that it was nothing about *her* that was holding him back. And he wanted her to understand him in a way that he'd never wanted before. He'd never opened up and talked about what had happened. But now he had been faced with the consequences of the choices he'd made so many years ago he wanted to acknowledge what he had felt, what he felt now.

'I want to explain. For you to understand. Look, it's not you, Lily.' He cringed when he heard for himself how clichéd that sounded. 'It's…it's Rosie. It's the way that you look at her. I won't ever have children, Lily. And I know that I cannot be in a relationship—any relationship—because of that.'

'Nic, we barely know each other. Don't you think that you're being—?'

He was thinking too far ahead. Of course he was. But if he didn't put an end to this now he wasn't sure how or if he ever could. What he had to say needed to be said out loud. He needed to hear it to make sure that he could never go back, never find himself getting closer to Lily and unable to get away.

'Maybe. Maybe I'm jumping to a million different conclusions here, and maybe I've got this all wrong. But the thing is, Lily, I'm never going to want to have children. Ever. And I don't think it would be right for me to leave you in any doubt about that, given your current situation.'

He allowed himself a quick look down at Rosie, and the painful clench of his heart at the sight of her round cheeks and intense concentration reminded him that he was doing the right thing. It was easier to say that it was because of the baby. Of course that was a big part of it. But there was more—there were things that he couldn't say. Things that he had been ashamed of for so long that he wasn't sure he could even bear to think of them properly, never mind share them with someone else.

'Well, thanks for telling me.'

She was fiddling with her coffee cup again, stirring it rapidly, sloshing some of the rich dark liquid over the side. He'd offended her—and what else did he expect, just telling half the story? All he'd basically done so far was break up with a woman he wasn't even dating.

'Lily, I'm sorry I'm not making much sense. It's just hard for me to talk about… The reason I don't want children…I was a father once. I lost my son, and it broke my heart, and I know that I can never put myself at risk of going through that again.'

And if she was going to take this gamble, raise her sister's child with no idea of what the future held, then she needed someone in her life she could rely on. Someone who would support her with whatever she needed. Who wouldn't let her down. He hadn't been able to do that when Max had died, hadn't been the man his partner had needed, and he'd lost his girlfriend as well as his son.

A hush fell between them and Nic realised he

had raised his voice until it was almost a shout. Lily dropped the bottle and Rosie gave a mew of discontent. But Nic's eyes were all on Lily, watching her face as she realised what he had said, as the significance of his words sank in.

She reached out and touched his hand. He should have flinched away. It was the reason he had told her everything, after all. But he couldn't. He turned his hand and grabbed hold of hers, anchoring himself to the present, saving himself from drowning in memories.

Now that he had told her, surely the danger was over. Now she would be as wary of these feelings as he was. He just wanted to finish this conversation—make sure that she knew that this wasn't personal, it wasn't about her. If Rosie had never turned up...if he'd never had a son... But there was no point thinking that way. No point in what-ifs and maybes.

'Nic, I'm so sorry. I don't know what to say, but I'd like to hear more about your son. If you want to talk about it.'

He breathed out a long sigh, his forehead pressed into the heels of his hands, but then he looked up to meet her gaze and she could see the pain, the loss, the confusion in his eyes.

'It won't change anything.'

She reached for his hand again, offering comfort, nothing more—however much she might want to.

'I know, but if you want to talk then I'd like to listen.'

He stared at the counter a little longer, until eventually, with a slight shake of his head, he started to speak.

'I was nineteen and naïve when I met this girl—

Clare—at a university party. We hit it off, and soon we were living in each other's pockets, spending all our time together. We were both in our first year, neither of us thinking about the future. We were having fun, and I thought I was falling in love with her.'

Lily was shocked at the strength of her jealousy over something that had happened a decade ago, and fought down the hint of nausea that his tale had provoked.

'Well, we were young and silly and in love, and we took risks that we shouldn't have.'

It didn't take a genius to see where this was going but, knowing that the story had a tragic end, Lily felt a pall of dread as she waited for Nic's next words.

'When Clare told me she was pregnant I was shocked. I mean, a few months beforehand we'd been living with our parents, and now we were going to be parents ourselves... But as the shock wore off we got more and more excited—'

His voice finally broke, and Lily couldn't help squeezing his hand. There was nothing sexual in it. Nothing romantic. All she wanted was to offer comfort, hope.

'By the time the baby was due we'd moved in together, even started to talk about getting married. So there I was: nineteen, as good as engaged, and with a baby on the way.'

His eyes widened and his jaw slackened, as if he couldn't understand how he had got from there to here—how the life that still lit up his face when he described it had disintegrated.

'The day Max was born was the best of my life. As soon as I held him in my arms I knew that I loved him. Everyone tells you that happens, but you never believe them until you experience it. He was so perfect, this tiny human being. For three weeks we were the perfect little family. I washed him, changed his nappies, fed him, just sat there and breathed in his smell and watched him sleep. I've never been so intoxicated by another person. Never held anything so precious in my arms.'

His face should have glowed at that. He should have radiated happiness, talking about the very happiest time of his life. But already the demons were incoming, cracking his voice and lining his face, and Lily held her breath, bracing herself.

'When he was three weeks old we woke one day to sunlight streaming into the bedroom and instantly knew that something was wrong. He'd not woken for his early feed. And when I went to his crib…'

He didn't have to say it. All of a sudden Lily wished that he wouldn't, that he would spare her this. But *he* hadn't been spared; *he* hadn't been shown mercy. He'd had his heart broken, his life torn apart in the most painful way imaginable. She couldn't make herself want to share that pain with him, but she wanted to help ease it if she could. She'd do just about anything to lift that blanket of despair from his face.

'He was gone. Already cold. I picked him up and shouted for Clare, held him in my arms until the ambulance arrived, but it was no good. Nothing I could have done would have helped him. They all told me that. They told me that for days and weeks afterwards. Until they started to forget. Or maybe they thought that *I* was forgetting. But I haven't, Lily.'

For the first time since he'd started speaking he

looked up and met her gaze head-on. There was solid determination there.

'I can never forget. And when I see Rosie…'

It all became clear: the way he turned away from the baby, the way he flinched if he had to interact with her, the stricken look on his face the one time he'd had to hold her. Seeing Rosie—seeing any baby—brought him unimaginable pain. There could be no children in his future, no family. And so she completely understood why it was he was fighting this attraction. Why he pushed away from their chemistry, trying to protect himself. Knowing that there could never be anything between them didn't make it easier, though. The finality of it hurt.

But there was one part of the story he hadn't finished.

'And…Clare?'

He dropped his head back into his hands and she knew that he was hiding tears. It was a couple of minutes before he could speak again.

'We were broken,' he said simply. 'We tried for a while. But whatever it was that had brought us together—it died with our baby. She needed… I couldn't…I saw her a couple of years ago, actually, in the supermarket, of all places, by the baked beans. We exchanged polite hellos, because what else could we say: *Remember when we lost our son and our world fell apart and could never be put back together? Remember when you needed me to be there for you, to help you through your grief, and I couldn't do it?'*

Lily choked back a sob. She couldn't imagine, never *wanted* to imagine, what this man had been through. She wanted to reach out and comfort him, to do anything she could to take his pain away, but she knew there was nothing to be done. Nothing that could undo what had happened, undo his pain. All she could do was be there for him, if that was what he wanted.

But it wasn't.

'So now you know why getting close to Rosie scares me—why getting close to you both can never happen. I can't go through that pain again, Lily. Just the idea of it terrifies me. How could I cope with another loss like that?'

Lily didn't have the answer to any of it. Of course she could say that the chances of it happening again were slim, but she couldn't promise it. No one could. And how could she blame him for wanting to spare himself that?

She didn't say anything when Nic stood from the table, only reached out a hand and rested it gently on his arm.

'Thank you,' she said. 'For everything. And I wish you all the best, Nic, I really do. I hope you can be happy again some day.'

CHAPTER FIVE

THREE WEEKS AFTER her sister had dropped her little surprise off on her doorstep Lily still hadn't heard anything from her. Social services seemed happy that Lily was being well cared for by her aunt, and were trawling through the appropriate paperwork. To begin with she'd thought it must be temporary, that one of these days Helen would call and ask for her daughter back. But so far—nothing.

And barely a word from Nic, either. Not that she had expected much after the way things had been left, but it was strange living with someone who could barely say more than good morning to her. A part of her had hoped, she supposed, that he might rethink things. That he might think that she—they—were worth taking a risk on. And then she remembered the look on his face when he told her about losing his son and knew that it couldn't happen. Knew that he wouldn't risk feeling like that again.

She lifted her head from the pillow and looked over at Rosie, still tucked in her crib, fast asleep again after her six o'clock feed. Lily listened to her breaths, to the steady whoosh of air moving in and out of her lungs. Rosie was the same age now as Nic's son had been when he died. After three weeks together, Lily could no longer imagine life without Rosie—couldn't imagine the pain of being torn from her.

So what would happen if Helen wanted her back? How could she keep mother and daughter apart, knowing how much it hurt to want a family and have them disappear from your life?

She collapsed back into her pillows and threw her arms over her face, blocking out the world, fed up with the circles her mind was spinning her in. She wanted to make sure that Helen was well and happy, but would that mean handing Rosie over? Accepting the fact that Helen might take off again, leaving her missing Rosie as she missed the rest of her family?

Much as she had tried to remember that she wasn't Rosie's mother, somewhere the line had become blurred. Because Helen hadn't just nipped to the shops, and Lily wasn't just being a helpful aunt: she was almost her legal guardian. It was Helen who had blurred this line, and Lily wasn't sure how she would cope if she suddenly turned everything on its head.

Thoughts still racing around her mind, she swung her legs out of bed and reached for her dressing gown. She'd learnt that if Rosie was sleeping she'd better shut her eyes, too, but this morning that was a luxury she couldn't afford. She had managed to put off a couple of her deadlines when she'd told her clients what had happened—sparing them most of the details—but she couldn't put them off for ever.

She had beta designs for two sites to finish, and while Rosie was sleeping she couldn't justify not working. Then there was the fact that she'd not bothered with the dishes last night, the fridge was looking decidedly bare, and when Rosie woke up she'd want milk, clean clothes and a clean nappy. The round of chores was endless, even with Nic's generosity, and she sometimes felt she'd been walking through fog since Rosie had arrived. A joyful fog, obviously, but an endlessly draining one, too.

She padded into the kitchen and hit the button on the kettle—still too foggy to attempt espresso—knowing that she needed coffee this morning, and wondering how breastfeeding mums coped with the newborn stage without caffeine. She felt as if she was flailing, barely keeping her head above water, and she wasn't even recovering from giving birth.

Over the rumbling of the kettle coming to the boil she heard her mobile ringing in the bedroom and ran to get it, hoping that she could reach it and hit 'silence' before it woke the baby.

When she got to it Rosie was already mewling quietly, and Lily scooped her up quickly before swiping to answer her phone.

'Hello?' she said, as quietly as possible, rocking Rosie in the vain hope that she'd decide to go back to sleep.

When her social worker told her the news she couldn't think of an answer. *Why* couldn't she think of an answer? So many times these past weeks she'd wondered how her sister was, whether she'd ever be ready to be part of a family again, and now here was the proof that she might want that one day. She wanted to see Lily—and her daughter—that morning.

'Okay,' she told the social worker eventually. 'I'll bring Rosie to her.'

As soon as she ended the call tears were threaten-

ing behind her eyes. Irrational tears? she wondered.
Through the sleep deprivation she was finding it hard
to remember what was reasonable and what wasn't. She
needed Kate and her no-nonsense way of seeing the
world, her way of cutting through the mess and making the world simple.

She dialled her number and waited, rocking slightly
on the bed. 'Come on, pick up…pick up…' She walked
back through to the kitchen as the ringing continued
on the other end of the phone. 'Come on, Kate. *Please*
pick up…'

'Everything okay?'

Not Kate. At the sound of Nic's voice she spun
around and the tears started in earnest, though she
couldn't rationalise why. Too much family drama. Too
little sleep.

'Any idea where your sister is?'

'Not sure,' he told her, and she could hear concern
for her in his voice. 'But I know that the Jackson case
is coming to trial this week. My guess would be cham-
bers or court. Is everything okay? Rosie?'

'She's fine,' Lily told him, though she couldn't stop
the tears.

She still clutched Rosie tight against her, her every
instinct telling her that she must protect the baby at all
costs. But protecting her didn't mean keeping her from
her own mother, if seeing her was what she wanted.

'Look, I've got to go out, but please can you find
Kate and tell her to meet me at the Sanctuary Clinic
as soon as possible?'

He paced the corridor of the clinic, asking himself for
the thousandth time what he was doing there. The sense

of déjà vu was almost overwhelming. It had been only a couple of weeks ago that he'd paced a similar corridor, asking himself a similar question.

Lily.

She had been the reason then, and she was the reason now. Her voice, so quiet and shocked, but filled with a fierce protectiveness for Rosie. *Find Kate*, she'd said.

But he hadn't been able to. When Kate was embroiled in a case there was no telling when she might emerge for sunlight and fresh air. All she could see was her duty to her client. Just as impossible as getting his sister on the phone was the thought of leaving Lily alone. She'd been so stoic, but he had heard the vulnerability in her voice and been unable to ignore it. The way she'd sounded—those intriguing layers of vulnerability and strength—had made him want to be here for her, *with* her. She could do this on her own, he had no doubt of that, but that didn't mean he wanted her to have to.

He was just relieved for now that Lily's sister was safe and well—he knew how much Lily had worried about her, how much she'd hoped to have her back in her life.

Lily emerged from the bathroom with Rosie smelling fresh, but there was a fearful look on her face. When they were halfway down the corridor, without thinking, he wrapped an arm around her. Holding her close to him, he could feel her body trembling.

'Here—' he gestured to some seats set against the wall '—do you want to sit for a minute? Get your breath? Helen's not going anywhere, and nor is Rosie.'

She sat in a chair and he pulled his arm back, suddenly self-conscious, aware of the line that he had crossed.

'Do you want to talk about it?'

Lily shook her head, but spoke anyway.

'Helen's been staying here since she left Rosie with me. She's not wanted to see us before now, but she's decided she's ready.'

'And you and Rosie—are *you* ready?'

She sat silent for a long moment. 'She's my sister. She's Rosie's mum. She's family. I don't want to lose her.'

'But you're the one making decisions for Rosie. Helen asked you to do that. If you're not ready...'

'*I'm* ready,' she said, with sudden steely determination. 'But I want to see Helen alone first, before I decide whether I'm ready for her to meet Rosie. I can't get hold of Kate and there's no one else. I know that I shouldn't ask. That after everything we've spoken about—'

'It's fine.' The words surprised him. He'd been all too ready to agree that she shouldn't ask, that it *was* too much, that he couldn't... But he'd looked down at Rosie, and he'd looked up at her aunt, and he'd known that this family had touched him. That Lily had touched him. And that much as he wanted to pretend he had never met them, that was impossible now.

It had been impossible from the moment he'd found Lily on her doorstep, babe in arms and already with a fierce determination to protect. It had been impossible when he'd laid out the hardest and most painful parts of his past, hoping that it would scare her off, hoping that the pain the conversation dredged up would be enough to scare *him* off. But it hadn't. He'd spent all that time questioning what he'd done. Wondering how he was going to live life full of the regret that he felt when he thought of Lily. Wondering if he could be brave enough to try and live another way.

And when he had reached out just now and taken her in his arms he'd had his answer. He didn't have a choice. The feelings he had for Lily weren't going to go away. Trying to convince her—convince himself— that they shouldn't do this hadn't made the pain less. It had made it worse. Walking away from Lily would leave another hole in a life that was already too empty.

'I'll watch her for you.'

'Are you sure?'

Her disbelief was written plainly on her face, and when he nodded he thought he saw a flash of hope there, of anticipation. He smiled in response—they had a lot to talk about later.

'We'll be fine. Your sister needs you now.'

Lily hesitated outside the door. She'd waited patiently for her sister to be ready, hoping every day that she would come back into their lives, but feeling terrified at the same time that she might ask for Rosie back, take her away. And then Lily would have lost a niece—almost a daughter—as well as her sister.

She took a deep breath and pushed open the door.

At the sight of her sister in the bed, pale and skinny, all her fears left her. As long as they were all safe and well, the rest of it didn't matter. She'd hoped so many times that she'd have a chance to reconnect with Helen. She couldn't be anything but pleased that she had somehow found her way back again.

'Lily?'

Lily hadn't realised that Helen was awake, but she reached out a hand to her with tears in her eyes.

'I'm so happy to see you,' she told her.

Helen sniffed, her expression cautious. 'I thought you might be angry.'

'I'm not angry—I've been so worried. I'm just glad that you're okay.'

'But what I did…'

'We don't need to talk about that now. The most important thing is to get you well again. Everything else we can talk about later.'

A tear slipped from the corner of Helen's eye and Lily wiped it away with a gentle swipe of her thumb.

'I knew that I couldn't look after her,' Helen went on, her tears picking up pace.

And even though Lily hushed her, told her that they didn't have to talk about it now, she carried on as if the words were backed up behind a failing dam and nothing could stop them surging forward.

'The house that I was living in—it wasn't safe. Not for me or her. And I couldn't think of another way, Lily. I knew that she'd be better off with you.'

'You did the right thing,' Lily reassured her. 'And your daughter's fine. She's doing really well.'

At that the dam finally broke, and Helen's face was drowned in tears.

'I…was…so…scared.' She choked the words out between sobs. 'After I left her with you I realised I couldn't go back to where I had been living, but I couldn't come home to you, either.'

'That's not true, Helen. You can come home any time. The house is yours just as much as it is mine. And I know that we both want what's best for Rosie.'

'Rosie?'

Lily gulped. She hadn't meant to use her name, knowing that she'd taken something of a liberty by choosing one in the first place. But there had been no one else to do it.

'If you don't like it…'

'No, it's perfect. I love it.' Helen's tears slowed. 'It just goes to show that I was right. You're the right person to look after her, Lily. I know that the way I did it wasn't right—just dumping her and running—but I didn't make a mistake. I can't be the one to raise her.'

Lily took a deep breath, feeling the thinness of the ice beneath her feet, knowing that one misstep could ruin her relationship with her sister for ever, could lose her Rosie.

'You've not been well,' she said gently. 'And you don't need to make big decisions right now or all at once. There'll be plenty of time to talk about this.'

Helen nodded, her features peaceful for the first time since Lily had arrived. 'I want to be part of her life—and yours, too, if you'll still have me. But I'm not going to change my mind. You're the best person to look after Rosie. I'm not ready to be a mother, Lily. I might never be. I'm not going to change my mind about this.'

Lily just squeezed her hand, lost for words.

'And maybe I will want to come home one day—but not yet, Lily. I can't do that until I'm really properly well, and that's going to take me some time.'

'I could—'

'I know you want to do everything for us, Lily. But you're already doing so much. I have to get better on my own, and I need space to do that.'

Space? How much space did she need? She'd given her nothing *but* space for years, and where had that got her? Living somewhere she didn't feel safe with a baby she couldn't care for.

'Will you do it? Will you take care of Rosie.'

There had never been any question about that.

'Of course I will. She's here, you know. If you'd like to see her.'

Pain crossed Helen's features for a moment. 'I thought I was ready, but…I'm not, Lily. It would hurt too much to see her. So what do you say? I'm not talking about a few weeks or months, Lily. I need to know that she'll be safe for *ever*. That I can concentrate on getting well without the pressure of… I know it's selfish.'

It wasn't. It might have been the most self*less* thing Lily had ever heard. Because the yearning and the love in Helen's face was clear. She hadn't abandoned Rosie because she was an inconvenience, or too much hard work, or because she cried too much. She'd done it because she loved her. She'd broken her own heart in order to give her child the best start in life, and Lily couldn't judge her for that.

'It's not selfish. And of course I'll take care of Rosie.' Her voice was choked as she said the words. 'I love her, Helen. You don't have to worry. I'll keep her safe.'

Some of the tension left Helen's body, and Lily could tell that she needed some of that space she'd been talking about.

She gave her hand another squeeze. 'I'll come back and visit again when you're ready. Rest now.'

'Thanks, sis,' Helen said, drifting off. 'You were always going to be an amazing mum.'

Back in the corridor, Lily leaned her forehead against the wall and took a couple of deep breaths, wanting to compose herself before she saw Rosie, not wanting her to sense that she had been upset.

She glanced down the corridor and saw that she was no longer in her car seat but on Nic's knee, being fed from a bottle. Lily couldn't help but smile. While she had been talking to her sister she'd almost forgotten that Nic had stayed, and the look on his face when she'd asked him to watch Rosie even though she'd known that she shouldn't. But the fear and the panic that she'd been expecting to see there hadn't emerged. Instead there had been something different, something new, and it had given her hope.

Now, seeing him holding the baby, she wondered what this meant. After everything that he'd said to her back at his flat, the harrowing story of his loss, she'd thought they'd said all that needed to be said about their feelings, their future. But here he was.

'Thank you so much for this,' she said as she reached the chairs and sat beside him. 'I can take her if you want.'

'She's fine. Let her finish her bottle.'

His words suggested that he was comfortable, but his body language was telling a different story. He was sitting bolt upright on the plastic chair, his shoulders and arms completely stiff. Rosie was more perched on him than snuggled against him, but that hadn't stopped her staring up at him with her big blue gaze locked onto his face as she fed.

I wish I could look at him like that, Lily thought. *With no need to hide what I feel, no need to look away when I realise that he's seen me.* How simple life must seem to Rosie, with no idea of the impact her birth had had on her whole family.

'How was it?' Nic asked her at last.

Lily blew out a breath. 'I don't really know—it's not like I have a lot to compare it to. But okay, I think.'

'That's good...'

'It's good that she wants to get better. But I wish she'd come home, that she'd let me take care of her. It's what I've been hoping for for years. But...'

'But you're worried about what will happen to Rosie if she gets well?'

She nodded, the lump in her throat preventing the words from coming.

'You know I can't tell you for definite what will happen.' The tone of his voice was soft and measured. 'But everyone involved will want what's best for Rosie.'

She nodded, still not trusting herself to speak.

At the beginning she had genuinely believed, when she'd said she would look after Rosie, that she was only taking care of her temporarily, until Helen was back and better. Now she couldn't imagine watching someone else sing her to sleep, someone else comfort her when she was upset. She was a little jealous just watching Nic giving her a bottle.

'So, are you heading home?' he asked when Rosie had finished.

'I thought I might walk through the park first, as the sun's out. I think me and Rosie need some fresh air. The smell of hospitals...'

'I'll walk with you, if that's okay?'

CHAPTER SIX

WALKING THROUGH THE PARK, just the three of them, Nic couldn't shake the feeling that he had wandered into someone else's life. To anyone else they would look like a family—a loving husband and wife, perhaps—taking a stroll with their baby, talking together, making plans for the future. This had been his life once, and it had left him so scarred that he had sworn he would never let himself come close to it again.

Until he had met Lily and been unable to forget her. And now was the moment he had to decide. It wasn't fair on Lily to keep pushing her away and then changing his mind. If he was going to take this chance, he had to commit to it.

'So…' he started as they exited the park. 'Have you got plans for dinner?'

She looked a little panic-stricken for a second.

'There're a few bits and pieces in the fridge. I was just going to rustle up something simple. Or maybe order something in…'

He could see the doubt in her eyes as she finally looked up at him, and he cursed himself for the confusion he must have caused her over the past days. He was more aware than anyone of how hot and cold he had blown. He wanted to reach out and smooth the lines of concern from her face. Instead he offered an encouraging smile, urging her to take a risk—as he had—and invite him in.

'We could order something together?' she suggested at last.

'I'd love to,' he agreed, opening the gate for her.

Back in the apartment, Nic reached across for another slice of pizza and asked the question that had been nagging at him since they had left the hospital.

'So, did your sister say anything about what her plans are...with Rosie?'

'It's still early days. I don't think she's really in a position to decide anything yet.' Lily took a long drink of her cola. 'But...'

'But?'

'She said that she wants me to take care of Rosie permanently. If I don't want to, or can't, I don't know what will happen. She'll go into care, I suppose.'

'And how do you feel about that?'

'About Rosie going into care?' She fought off a wave of panic and nausea, reminding herself that the social worker had told her that they tried their hardest to keep families together. That Rosie being taken away completely would be a last resort. 'Honestly, the thought of it makes it hard to breathe.'

Nic looked at her closely and she dropped her eyes, not enjoying the depth of his scrutiny, feeling as if he was seeing all too much of her.

'There must be a lot of fantastic foster parents out there. And couples waiting to adopt. All you ever hear on the news is the horror stories, but every type of family has those. I'm sure that Rosie would find a happy home if that's what you and Helen decide is best.'

Lily shook her head, not trusting herself to speak for a moment. After a long breath, she chose her words carefully. 'But she should be with her family. I *have* to look after her.'

'Why do I feel there's more to this story?' Nic asked.

'What do you mean? I just want to take care of my family.'

'It's not all your responsibility.'

He was using his careful voice again, and she read the implication in that loud and clear. He thought she was being irrational, that she needed talking down like some drunk about to lose her temper. Well, if he carried on like this…

'It's okay to admit that maybe sometimes you need help.'

'I don't need help to look after my niece, thank you very much. I'm sorry if that's not what you want to hear. If you were hoping that maybe I'd wake up one day soon unencumbered by a baby. It's not exactly what I had in mind for the next few years, but she's my responsibility and I'm not handing her over to strangers.'

He held his hands palms up and sat back on his stool, surprise showing in his raised eyebrows and baffled expression. 'Whoa! I'm sorry, Lily. That's not what I meant at all. I'm not going to lie and say that Rosie doesn't make things complicated, but I'd never expect you to give her up. I'd never want that.'

'Then what *do* you want? Because I've got to tell you I'm struggling to keep up. The last time we talked you were very clear that I was nothing more to you than a temporary lodger—and not even a very welcome one at that. But now here we are, strolling through the park and sharing dinner. Why?'

She hadn't meant to get mad at him, but he'd already squashed her every romantic and X-rated fantasy, when she'd only just started to realise the feelings she was developing, and it was suddenly all too much. She'd held back before—keeping her feelings at the back of her mind, not questioning his—and she'd had enough. They were both grown-ups. If he was man enough to have these feelings then he'd damn well better be man enough to talk about them.

'Because I can't make myself *not* want this. And I've tried, Lily. I've tried for both of us. Because I'm not the right guy for you. I've tried to keep my distance because I know that this isn't good for either of us—I can't be the person you need me to be. But something keeps throwing us back together and I don't know if I can fight it any more.'

Man enough, then.

Lily froze with a slice of pizza halfway to her mouth. Complete and utter honesty was what she had been hoping for, but really the last thing she'd been expecting. The raw power of his words made her want to move closer and pull away at the same time. He'd just told her that he wasn't sure he was ready. He was taking a big gamble with her feelings and with his, and she wasn't sure that was a game she wanted to play. Had he really thought this through?

'I'm not sure, Nic. I barely have the time or the brain capacity to think beyond the next bottle and nappy-change. I'm not sure that I can even *think* about a relationship. And you know me and Rosie come as a package deal, right? I don't know what's going to happen with Helen in the future. I don't know whether I'll be Rosie's caregiver for the next week, the next month, or the rest of her life. There are no guarantees either way.'

She let out a long, slow breath.

'I'm sorry, but I don't think I can even consider a relationship right now. If you want to be friends, I'd like that.'

He gave her a long, searching look, before sighing. 'Of course. You're right. But friends sounds good. I'd like that.'

'That's exactly what I need.' She offered him a small, tentative smile, feeling her hackles gradually smooth.

'I guess I could take that as a compliment. But how about we leave off over-analysing getting to know each other and change the subject? If we're going to be friends, then talking over pizza and a glass of wine seems like something we should master.'

'Agreed. So, Dominic Johnson, in the spirit of getting to know each other, tell me something about you I don't already know. Please, let's talk about something completely normal for a change.'

She took a bite of her pizza while she waited for him to reply, trying to make her body relax. Instead all it was interested in was Nic—his smell, his nearness, the fact that he was tearing down barriers she'd been counting on for weeks.

'There's not really much to tell.'

His words snapped her attention back, and she listened intently, trying to school her resistant body.

'I grew up with Mum and Dad and Kate in the suburbs of Manchester. Completely unremarkable childhood. Kate and I still get dragged back there regularly for family Sunday lunches.'

'Sounds lovely,' Lily said. She *knew* it was lovely, actually, and had been up there with Kate more than once. 'You're lucky,' she told Nic.

He nodded in agreement. 'How about you?'

Lily took a deep breath, realising too late that of course her question had been bound to lead to this. In wanting to hear something completely unremarkable about his life she'd led them to talking about the most painful parts of hers.

'Uh-uh.' She shook her head as she reached for the last dough ball, wondering how best to deflect his question. 'I'm not done grilling you.'

She thought around for a topic of conversation that wouldn't lead back to her family, and her failure to hold things together at the heart of it.

'How did you start your charity? Why did you decide that you wanted to spend your life improving the conditions of child factory workers? It seems like a bit of a leap the suburbs.'

He smiled softly, obviously resigned to being the subject of her questioning for now.

'It never really seemed like a choice. I travelled after…after Max, and I was horrified by some of the things that I saw. I had nothing to come home to—or that's what it felt like at the time—so I stayed and tried to do something about it.'

'And was it what you expected?'

'It was worse—and better,' he replied. 'I saw things that I wish I could forget, and I saw people's lives saved because of my work. But what I loved most was that it was so all-consuming. It exhausted me physically and mentally. It didn't leave room for me to think about anything else. It was exactly what I needed.'

'And now? Is it still all-consuming?' Because there wasn't room for anyone else in what he'd just described.

'It can be on the days I want it to be,' he said, thoughtfully and with a direct look. 'There've been a few of those lately... But usually, no, it doesn't have to be. That's part of the reason I took the job in London. I knew that I couldn't carry on the way I had been. And I knew that my parents wanted me to be closer to home. I've spent the last ten years trying to change these companies from the outside—I thought trying from the inside might work better.'

She watched him closely, wondering whether she had been part of the reason he'd needed a distraction lately. Or was it just his grief he didn't want to face?

She sat back on her stool and rubbed her belly as Nic eyed the last slice of pizza speculatively. 'I'm done,' she declared. 'It's all yours.'

They fell into an easy silence as Nic ate, and Lily smiled up at him, feeling suddenly shy, and also shattered. Rosie's feeds through the night and her early starts were catching up with her, and much as she was loath to admit it suddenly all she could think about was her duvet, her pillow, and the fact that Rosie would be awake and hungry almost before she managed to get to them.

For half a second she thought about Nic being under that duvet with her, about seeing his head on the pillow when she woke in the morning.

Something of her thoughts must have shown on her face, because Nic raised an eyebrow.

'What?' he asked. 'What did I miss?'

'Nothing!' Lily declared, far too earnestly. 'Nothing...'

'Something,' Nic stated, watching her carefully. 'But if you don't want to share that's fine.'

'Good. Because your reverse psychology doesn't work on me.'

Nic laughed. 'Busted. I want to know what you were thinking!'

'And I'm not going to tell.'

He looked triumphant at that. 'Well, then, I'll choose to interpret that look however I want to, and there's nothing you can do about it.'

Lily shook her head, laughing. 'Right, that's enough.' She stood good-naturedly, clearing away the pizza box and their glasses. 'I'm going to bed.'

He walked through to the hall with her, and she hesitated outside her door.

'This was nice,' she said eventually, feeling suddenly nervous, unable to articulate anything more than that blatant understatement.

He grinned, though, his smile lighting his whole face. Maybe he'd heard all the things she hadn't said.

'I'm glad we talked.'

So he could do understatement too. On purpose? Or was he feeling awkward as well?

Lily reached for the door handle, but as her hand touched cold metal warm skin brushed her cheek, and she drew in a breath of surprise. Nic nudged her to look up at him as he took a step closer. The heat of his body seemed to jump the space between them, urging her closer, flushing her skin. She looked up and met his gaze. His eyes swam with a myriad of emotions.

Desire, need, relief, hope… All were reflected in her own heart. But they couldn't have timed this worse. She'd meant what she said earlier. Friendship was all she had space for in her life.

She closed her eyes as she stretched up on tiptoe and let her lips brush against his cheek. Soft skin rasped against sharp stubble and for a moment she rested her cheek against his, breathing in his smell, reminding herself that even if she did drag him inside to her bed she'd be snoring before he even got his shirt off.

Nic's other hand found the small of her back and pressed her gently to him, appreciative rather than demanding. She let out a long sigh as she dropped her forehead to his shoulder, and then finally turned the door handle.

'Goodnight…?'

There was still the hint of a question in Nic's farewell, and she smiled.

'Goodnight.'

CHAPTER SEVEN

HE BARELY HAD a foot through the front door when Lily
flew past him. Shirtless and running.

'Everything okay?' he called to her retreating back,
knowing that he should drag his eyes away from the
curve of her waist and the smoothness of her skin, but
finding that his moral compass wasn't as refined as
he'd always hoped. There was something about the
way the light played on her skin, the way it seemed to
glow, to luminesce…

'I'm sorry,' she called over her shoulder as she ran
into her bedroom. 'Spectacular timing. I'll be right
out.'

Rosie was in a bouncy chair in the kitchen, wearing
most of her last bottle, he guessed, and had clearly been
hastily and inadequately mopped up by the kitchen roll
on the counter. Lily turned suddenly and he threw his
gaze away—anywhere but at her. His mind was filled
by the image of her bare skin, the sweep of her shoulder, the curve of her…

No. To ogle a shoulder was one thing, but there were
lines he shouldn't cross.

Instead he went into the kitchen and looked at Rosie
and at the dribble of milk trickling down her chin. With

mock exasperation he grabbed a muslin square and started mopping. He kept it objective, detached. There was no need to pick her up, but it wasn't really fair to leave her damp and uncomfortable, either. If he was going to be spending more time with Lily, he couldn't ignore Rosie completely.

Lily emerged a moment later, pulling down a T-shirt to cover that last inch of pale flesh above her jeans.

'Thanks for doing that. I started, but I seemed to be getting messier from trying to clean her up. Seemed one of us should be clean, at least.'

'It's no problem,' he said, holding out the muslin, handing back responsibility. His eyes were fixed just above her T-shirt, where shoulder met collarbone and collarbone met the soft skin of her neck.

And then it was hidden behind Rosie's soft-haired head and he was forced to look away again. He wondered how he could pinch Rosie's spot, how he could get his lips behind Lily's ear, breathe in her smell as Rosie was doing.

For another whole week, while he'd been putting in fourteen-hour days at the office, all he'd had to remember was that brief kiss on the cheek, the press of her soft warm skin against his, the fruity scent of her shampoo and the heat that had travelled from her body to his without them even touching. The long nights had been filled with plans he knew would never be fulfilled: for picking up where that kiss had left off, for having her cheek against his again, but this time turning her, finding her mouth with his, scooping her up in his arms and heading straight for her bedroom, or the couch, or the kitchen table…

'I'm so sorry. I know I said I'd cook tonight, but

I haven't got started on dinner yet,' she said, bouncing Rosie and trying to snatch up tissues and muslins from the kitchen counter and shuffling dirty pots from the breakfast bar. 'I just don't know what happens to the hours.'

Rosie was showing no sign of settling, so he grabbed ingredients from the fridge and tried to fire his imagination.

'You don't have to do that,' she told him, still bouncing and rocking. 'I'll be on it in just a minute.'

'Don't worry—let me,' he insisted. 'I like to cook.'

She looked up at him in surprise. 'Hidden depths?'

He took a few steps closer to her, pulled the muslin from her hand and stopped her rocking for just a minute. For the first time since that too-brief kiss on the cheek she met his eyes, and he relaxed into her gaze.

'There's a lot you don't know.'

She wanted to find out, she realised. She wanted his secrets.

'I'm pretty sure that you'd rather not arrive home to a strange woman in your apartment, baby spit-up, no sign of dinner, and—'

'It's not so bad,' he said with a grin.

It was true, he realised as he spoke. And he wanted her any way she came—baby spit-up and all. Because for this scene to be any different, *she* would have to be different. *Not* the sort of woman who took in a vulnerable child. *Not* the sort of woman who put feeding that child before her own appearance. He wanted her just as she was.

He looked down at the top of Rosie's head, at the way she was nuzzling against Lily's shoulder, the way she'd started to snuffle again since he'd stopped

Lily moving. If he wanted her to be that woman, if he wanted to be *with* that woman, then he was going to have to learn to be patient. If these few weeks had taught him anything, it was how to wait for Lily.

'She needs you,' he said. 'I'll look after dinner. And then, when she's sleeping, we can…'

She looked up again, this time with a blush and a smile.

'We can eat. And talk.'

The smile spread into a grin—and a knowing one at that.

He started chopping an onion, and had to bat away Lily's one-handed attempts to help. Ten minutes later he had a sauce bubbling on the stove, and had to snatch the wooden spoon from Lily's hand as she attempted to stir it.

'Did you never hear the one about too many cooks? Out.' He threatened her clean T-shirt with the sauce-covered spoon until he could close the door behind her.

Finally, after she'd popped her head around the door twice, just to 'check' there was nothing she could do, they had Rosie asleep in her Moses basket and dinner on the table. Conversation flowed easily between them as he shared stories of his client meetings, and told her about his plans for the new product lines he'd like to stock. They talked about what she'd been up to, but she managed to deflect most of his questions.

He wondered how much of it was her trying to protect him, shielding him from Rosie because she knew the baby caused him pain.

He couldn't remember which of them had suggested watching a movie, but now, in the dark, sharing a couch with her, he wanted to curse whoever it had been.

He felt like a teenager again. Even their choice of a comedy, hoping to steer clear of the romantic, seemed hopelessly naïve. And, like the awkward fifteen-year-old he vaguely remembered being once, he was thinking tactics. How to break their silence and separation? Trying to guess whether she was watching the film or if—like his—her line of thought was on something rather different.

They had agreed to be just friends, but his week of long days in the office—giving her the space she needed—had proved to him that keeping his feelings friendly was going to be anything but easy. Especially knowing that she was attracted to him too. She hadn't denied that before, after all. Only said that the timing wasn't right. Well, when was it *ever* right? Had she missed him, too, this week? Rethought their very grown-up and very gruelling decision to keep things platonic?

As he glanced across at her Lily turned to him, lips parted and words clearly on the tip of her tongue.

'I was just going to…to get a drink. Do you want anything from the kitchen?'

Her cheeks were rosy again, and he wondered if that was really what she had planned on saying. But most importantly she'd hit 'pause' on the movie, broken the stalemate. He watched her retreat to the kitchen and relaxed back into the cushions of the sofa. How was he meant to make it through the rest of this movie? It was torture. Pure torture. She *must* be feeling this tension as much as he was. Was she as intrigued by the attraction between them as he?

She emerged from the kitchen with a couple of glasses, balancing a plate of cakes. She'd pulled her hair back, exposing even more of the soft skin of her neck, and it took every ounce of his self-control not to sneak his arm along the back of the sofa until his hand found it, touched it. He knew that if he did his whole experience of the world would be reduced to the very tips of his fingers, and he'd be able to think about nothing other than how much he wanted her.

Her face was turned up to his, and when he breathed in it was all *her*, fruity and fresh. She smiled, and the sight of it filled him with resolve. She didn't want more than this. He would never be everything she needed in a partner, a husband. They were doing the right thing.

But when he closed his eyes he imagined her hand on his jaw, pulling him close, her tongue teasing, him opening his mouth to her and taking control. One hand would wind in her hair, tilting her head and caressing her jaw. He could practically hear her gasp as he pulled her into his lap. He knew the sound would reach his bones.

But even in his fantasy there was something else: a hesitancy, a caution that he couldn't overcome. He opened his eyes to find her watching him from the other end of the couch. He knew that his fantasy was written on his face, and other parts of his body.

'Nic...'

'Don't,' he said, holding up a hand to stop her. 'Nothing's changed since last time we talked about this. Apart from the fact that I've not been able to stop thinking about you... But it doesn't matter. We're doing the right thing. I know that. One of these days Rosie's going to need a dad—or a father figure, at least. You'll meet someone amazing who can give you the family life you deserve.'

He could never be that man.

'It's been a long week,' he told her, faking a yawn. 'I think I'm going to hit the sack.'

And with that he left her, staring after him as he practically ran from the room.

CHAPTER EIGHT

'Right then, miss. Are you going to tell me what's going on? Because Nic is being annoyingly discreet. I don't know what's got into him.'

'And I have no idea what you're talking about.'

'Oh, like hell you don't. The pair of you have been making doe eyes at each other since the day he pitched up on your doorstep. I can forgive *him* not telling me what's going on: he's my brother, and a bloke, and he has been irritating me for as long as I can remember. It's like a vocation for him. But you're my best friend and you have a new man in your life and you're telling me *nothing*. That's just not acceptable by anyone's standards of friendship.'

Lily groaned as she tipped the pram back and lifted it onto the pavement. 'A nice walk in the park,' Kate had said. 'Fresh air and a catch-up,' Kate had said. Since Rosie had landed they'd barely had the chance for more than a hello. It was her own fault for not re-alising that what she'd actually meant was *I will be grilling you for details about my brother*.

Well, if that was what she wanted…

'Okay, if it's details about the wild, sweaty sex I've been having with your brother you want you should have said. I hope you've got all afternoon free, though. Because that boy has stamina—and imagination.'

Kate's squeal had an elderly couple by the pond swivelling to stare at them and pigeons taking off from the path.

'That is all kinds of disgusting. I don't want details. But the fact that you've been doing the dirty with my brother and not telling me...*that* we need to talk about.'

Lily laughed at the look of horror on Kate's face. 'Calm it down, Kate. There has been no dirty. I'm winding you up.'

'You're— Oh, I'm going to kill you. *And* him. I've not decided yet which I'm going to enjoy more. So there's nothing going on?'

'Nothing.'

It was absolutely the truth. The fact that they were both *thinking* about what might be going on was beside the point.

'Then why are you blushing?'

Damn her pale skin—always getting her into trouble.

'I know that he likes you.'

Lily took a deep breath. 'I know he does too. But it's more complicated than that.'

'You don't like *him*?'

'Of course I like him. You've met your brother, right? Tall, good-looking, kind—all "I have a brilliant business brain but I choose to use it saving the world"?'

'Then what's the problem?'

What was the problem? There was the fact that she'd just become solely responsible for raising a brand-new human without even the usual nine-month notice period. There was the fact that Nic was still so scarred from losing his own son that he couldn't look at Rosie without flinching. There was the fact that she fell asleep any time she sat down for more than six minutes at a time, and the fact that her life was threatening to overwhelm her. It was hard to imagine how anything more complicated with Nic *wouldn't* push her over the edge.

And there was more that he hadn't told her. It wasn't just Rosie he was fighting. When he looked at Lily she saw something else—doubt. He'd told her that he wasn't the right man for her, but she failed to see why. Not wanting a life with a baby in it was one thing, but there was more to it than that. He warned her away whenever they got close, as if he couldn't trust himself.

What really tipped the situation over from difficult to impossible was the fact that she didn't want to care about any of that. That all the time she was walking around sleep-deprived and zombified her thoughts went in one direction only—straight to Nic.

'We're just friends—it's all we can handle right now. Honestly, Kate, if there was more to tell you I would. But we're still trying to work it out ourselves.'

Kate gave her a long look, but then her face softened and Lily knew that she was backing down and the grilling was over—for now, at least.

'And how are things with Rosie. Any word from Helen?'

'Nothing more yet—only that she's still at the clinic and doing well. Social services are happy with how things are going with Rosie, so it looks like this is it. Once they've decided Helen's well enough to make a final decision I guess we'll have more paperwork to do.'

'And you're still sure you're making the right decision?'

'I can't see what other decision I could make. She's my family. We should be together.'

Kate gave her a long look. 'I know you miss your mum, and your sister, but that doesn't mean—'

Lily stopped walking and held up a hand to stop Kate. 'Please—don't. I promise you I've thought about this. I've asked myself again and again if I'm doing the right thing and I honestly believe that I am. I *want* to do this. I love Rosie, and we're having a great time.'

'Well, she *is* completely adorable. I can't blame you—totally worth turning your life upside down for.'

Lily looked down at the pram, where Rosie had been sleeping soundly for over an hour. When she was like this, how could she disagree?

She'd just got the baby fed, changed and sleeping when the front door opened. She backed out of the bedroom on tiptoes, holding her breath to avoid waking Rosie. Nic was standing in the hall, bearing a bunch of flowers and a grin.

'Hi.'

He bent forward to kiss her on the cheek—strictly friendly—and she sneakily soaked up the smell of his aftershave and the warmth of his body.

'Hi, yourself. You look good. Did you do something different with your hair?'

She knew for a fact that there was milk in her hair, and that she'd pulled on this T-shirt from where she'd tossed it by the side of the bed last night. What a gentleman.

'How was it?' Lily asked as they walked through

to the kitchen. 'Did you manage to clear your desk for rest of the weekend?'

He'd been working and travelling non-stop since he'd arrived back in London, and had declared last night that he was ready for a break. He'd suggested a touristy day, sightseeing, and had volunteered *her* as tour guide.

'All sorted. I'm free till Monday morning. Are you still on for today?' He thrust the flowers at her. 'I'm banking on you saying yes, and these are a thank-you in advance.'

Lily thought about it—a few hours in the sunshine in one of the parks, perhaps the Tower of London or the London Eye to really up the cheesy tourist factor.

'Of course we're still on. Do I have time to change?'

'An hour before the car arrives. Is that enough? I can always call and delay.'

'An hour's perfect.'

She left Nic in the kitchen while she dived into the shower and grabbed jeans and a clean shirt. Rosie didn't stir in her crib, and Lily kept an eye on the clock, wondering when she'd wake for her next feed. She'd been sleeping for an hour already, which meant that she'd be waking up…just as the car reached them. *Not* perfect, then—far from it.

Maybe she should just tell Nic that they needed to leave a little later—but he'd seen too much of her struggling already, and she didn't want to admit that an hour wasn't enough time to get two people ready and out of the house. She'd just have to wake Rosie early from her sleep and feed her before they set off. Hopefully she'd pop straight off back to sleep afterwards.

Clean from the shower, Lily headed back out to the

kitchen, to find Nic immersed in stacking the dish-washer.

'Nic! You shouldn't! Leave those and I'll do them when we get back.'

'It's no problem,' he insisted as Lily gathered up sterilised bottles and cartons of ready-mixed formula, trying to work out how many bottles they would need to get them through the day.

Nic finished the washing up, despite her contin-ued protests, and with twenty minutes to go until the car arrived the kitchen was looking more like a home than a bomb site.

'Right, then—anything else I can do to help?' Nic asked.

'Absolutely not. I just need to give Rosie a quick feed and then we're all good.'

She cracked open the curtains in the bedroom slightly—just enough so that it wouldn't feel like night to Rosie—and then lifted her from the crib, tickling her fingers up and down her spine and over the soles of her feet. When her eyes started to open Lily moved her face closer and smiled at her, holding eye contact.

'Morning, sleepyhead,' she crooned. 'Time for some-thing to eat, and then we're going on an adventure!'

She swiped a bottle from the kitchen on her way, and then settled into a big comfy chair in the living room, where Nic had turned on some music.

'So, am I allowed to know what's in store for us today?' Lily asked once Rosie had started to feed.

'I can tell you if you really want to know, but I thought a surprise…'

Lily grinned. She couldn't remember the last time someone had organised a surprise for her, and after weeks of being enslaved to a demanding newborn, the thought of being spoilt for the day was irresistible.

'A surprise sounds divine. Though I'm not sure how I'm meant to play tour guide if I don't know where we're going.'

'Without giving too much away, let's just say that you don't have to worry too much about that. You're doing enough, indulging my need to see the tourist hotspots. I don't expect you to sing for your supper, too.'

Lily was distracted by Rosie spitting out the bottle, but managed to rearrange the muslin square before she got a direct hit on her clean shirt. She tried to get her to take the bottle again, but she turned her head and pursed her lips. Lily gave a small sigh. Perhaps choosing this morning to try waking her for a feed for the first time wasn't the best idea she'd ever had—it seemed Rosie wasn't a big fan of spontaneity.

She sat her up and rubbed between her shoulder-blades, hoping that she just had some wind and could be persuaded to take the rest of her bottle.

'Everything okay?' Nic asked, when she gave a small huff of exasperation.

'Just fussing,' Lily told him, not wanting to admit that her mistake was probably to blame.

'There's no hurry, you know. We can move the car back.'

'It's fine—honestly.' The damage had been done now, after all.

She offered Rosie the bottle again, but she absolutely refused it, and Lily knew that she was being unfair on her when all she wanted to do was sleep. Cursing whatever instinct it was that had kept her quiet when she could so easily have asked Nic to change their plans, she rocked the baby back to sleep and wondered when she'd wake next—when she'd be hungry next. She couldn't shake the feeling that she'd just played Russian roulette with their day.

The doorbell rang just as Rosie dropped off and Lily held her breath for a moment, wondering if the sound would wake her, but it seemed they'd got away with it. She lowered her gently into her car seat and hefted her to the hallway—for a tiny bundle she was certainly starting to feel like a heck of a weight to carry around.

Nic answered the door to a driver in a smart-looking uniform, and for a second Lily was surprised. She'd heard 'car' and thought local minicab, but it seemed Nic's idea of a day's sightseeing might be somewhat different to her own. She glanced down at the plimsolls she'd been about to pull on and wondered whether she ought to go for something smarter.

'Should I change?' she asked Nic. 'I'm in the dark about what we're doing, but if I need to be...'

'You look perfect as you are,' he told her, and she smiled, but still wasn't entirely at ease.

Lily watched out of the window as they headed down towards the river, trying to work out where they were going. They zoomed past a couple of parks, which ruled those out, and by the time they pulled up at a wharf Lily had to admit defeat. She had no idea where they were going.

'We're here?' she asked Nic, and he grinned by way of an answer. 'What are we doing?'

'Wait and see,' he told her with child-like enthusiasm. 'But it should be amazing.'

She pulled Rosie's car seat out and looked up at

Nic, hoping for some guidance. He nodded towards the water, where a sleek white and silver yacht was moored.

'Are we going aboard?' she asked.

'We are indeed.'

He was practically bouncing now—and no wonder. The yacht was magnificent—all flowing lines and shiny chrome, and decks scrubbed to within an inch of their lives. She could see through the expanse of glass that a dining room had been set with sparkling crystal and polished silverware. It looked as if they were in for a treat.

'Would you like the pram, madam?' the driver asked as he opened the boot of the car.

She glanced at the gangplank and the yacht's decks, and for a shivery moment had visions of a runaway pram rolling towards the railings that edged the decks.

'I think I'll take the sling instead.'

Nic grabbed the changing bag from the boot and hefted it to his shoulder. Climbing up onto the gangplank, he held out a hand to her. As his fingers closed around her palm warmth spread through her hand, and she had to remind herself sternly of the very sensible decision that they'd both taken to remain just friends. But with the fancy dining room and the glamorous yacht this was starting to look more like a date than temporary flatmates hanging out for the afternoon.

'Welcome, sir, madam—and to the little one. You're very welcome on board. Luncheon will be served in thirty minutes. In the meantime feel free to explore the decks or take a drink in the champagne bar on the upper deck.'

Lily smiled at the man as he discreetly retreated

from them, though she couldn't help a little twist of anxiety. Luncheon, champagne bar... She'd had take-away sandwiches in mind when Nic had first mentioned something to eat and sightseeing, and she wondered if he had higher expectations of the day than he'd let on. This was looking less and less like a casual day out and more like a seduction.

She looked up at Nic, wondering whether she'd glean any clue from his expression. But his beaming smile didn't give much away.

'Nic, this is amazing,' she said. 'If a little unex-pected...'

'I know...I know. It's a bit over the top. But I wanted to see London from the water, and my new assistant said the food on board was not to be missed. There's nothing wrong with treating ourselves, is there?'

She searched for double meanings, but found none in his words or in his eyes. She was worrying about nothing. It was no surprise, really. After he'd ended up cooking for them both these last few weeks, he wanted a slightly more refined dining experience.

'So, what will it be?' he asked. 'Exploring or the champagne bar?'

Lily thought about it for a second, measuring the rocking of the boat under her feet and the weight of the baby in her arms. 'Exploring, I think,' she said with a smile.

They walked the decks, gasping over the unrivalled luxury of the vessel, the attention to detail and the de-votion to function and aesthetics in every line. Pol-ished chrome and barely there glass provided a barrier between them and the water, but as they climbed step after step Lily's head grew dizzier and her feet a little less steady.

When she had to pause for a moment, at the top of the highest step, Nic gave her a concerned look. 'You okay?' he asked, with a gentle arm around her shoulder.

'Fine,' she told him, shrugging off his arm.

It was making it too hard to think, and she needed to focus all her energy on keeping herself on her feet at the moment.

Nic's face fell—just for a second, before he caught it—and she knew that she had hurt his feelings. She'd opened her mouth, without being entirely sure what she would say, when a liveried steward came up the steps behind them and asked that they take their seats in the dining room. With just a quick glance at Nic, Lily shot down the stairs, glad of the moment to clear her head.

It wasn't that she hadn't wanted Nic's support. God knew it had felt good to have his arm around her. But there was the problem. It was *too* good. It would be too easy to forget all the very sensible, grown-up reasons that they were staying friends and friends only. And it wasn't as if Nic had meant anything by it; he'd just been trying to help when he'd seen that she needed it. It was her overactive libido that was complicating things—having her jumping like a cat every time he came near her.

There were about a dozen tables in the dining room, each set for two with a shining silver candelabra and fresh-cut roses in crystal.

'Wow,' Nic said behind her. 'This is…'

She turned round to look at him, not sure how to interpret the wavering in his voice.

Go on, she urged him silently. Because this dining room had 'romance' written all over it, and right now she was struggling. Struggling to see how they were meant to stay friends if Nic was going to spring romance on her with no warning. Struggling to know what he wanted from her if this was where he thought they were in their 'friendship'.

'This is…unexpected,' he said.

The candlelight made it hard to tell, but she was sure there was a little more colour in his cheeks than normal. She let out a sigh of relief. Okay, so she was worrying over nothing. This wasn't some grand seduction—just a lunch that was turning out to be a little more romantic than either of them had been expecting.

Lily watched the other diners taking their seats as they were shown to a table by the window, tucked into a corner of the room. Light flooded in through the floor-to-ceiling windows, throwing patterns and shapes from the crystal and the flatware.

Nic tucked the changing bag under the table as they sat, and Lily reached down to adjust Rosie in her carrier. She'd slept through their tour of the vessel and Lily glanced at her watch, not sure what time she would wake.

Nic looked determinedly out of the window, Lily noticed, and was careful to make sure that his eyes never landed on Rosie.

'Come on, then,' he said, gesturing at the window. 'What are we looking at? I can't waste the fact that I'm out here with a genuine Londoner.'

'How have you never been sightseeing in London?' she asked with wonder. 'Never mind the fact that your sister has lived here for years, you've been to —what?—six different cities in the past couple of

months alone. You don't honestly need me to point
out the OXO Tower, do you?'

'And in not one of those other cities did I have a tour
guide. Or time off for lunch, for that matter. What can
I say? Maybe I've packed in too much work and not
enough fun.'

'Well, we'll make today all about fun, then. What
else have you got planned for us?'

'Nope—still not telling.'

She laughed, and then looked down as she felt Rosie
rubbing her head against her chest, a sure sign that she
was about to wake up and demand a bottle. She was
just going to suggest that they find a way to heat up
some formula when the maître d' appeared.

Seemed everybody was ready to eat.

As a team of waiting staff paraded into the dining room, carrying their starters, Lily dug through her
bags and found a bottle and a carton of ready-mixed
formula.

'Excuse me,' she said to their waitress, once she'd
placed their starters in front of them, 'could I have
some hot water to heat a bottle?'

The girl shot Rosie a look that was fifty per cent
fear of the baby and fifty per cent disdain. It turned
out that diners under one weren't exactly flavour of the
month on luxury restaurant cruises.

'Is she okay?' Nic asked, as Rosie started to mewl
like a mildly discontented kitten.

'Just hungry, I think,' Lily said, rubbing her back
and trying to get her to settle.

If only her fusspot of a niece would take a cold
bottle—but she had tried that before, with no success.
She tried again now anyway, hoping that maybe she'd

be hungry enough not to care, but after screwing up her face she spat out a mouthful of milk and Lily knew they had no choice but to wait for the hot water. She really ought to get one of those portable bottle warmers...

The doors to the dining room swung open, and Lily looked up, hoping to see a steaming pot of water heading her way. Instead the waitress was carrying bottles of wine, topping up the glasses on the table nearest the kitchen. Rosie chose that moment to let out a scream, and every head in the room turned towards her—Nic's included.

'I think maybe I should take her out... Just for a few minutes...until she settles.'

'If you think that's best,' Nic replied, his expression hovering somewhere around concerned. 'Is there anything I can do?'

'If you could get that bottle warm, that would be amazing. Sure you don't mind?'

She'd have done it herself—marched into the kitchen and found a kettle—but from the looks she was getting a hasty retreat seemed like the safer option.

'Course. I'll grab someone. Want me to bring it out to you? Or will you come back in?'

She should have an answer to that. But all she could think was, What was he asking *her* for? *He* was the one who'd done this before—*he* was the one with experience of being a parent, having had months to prepare for it and classes to learn about it.

But she couldn't ask him about any of that.

She pushed through the heavy door and went out onto the deck, taking in a deep lungful of breeze and spray. She let the breath out slowly, her eyes closed, focussing on calming thoughts, knowing that it would help Rosie settle.

Could everyone still hear her? She risked a glance at the windows. Whether they could hear her or not, she was still providing the entertainment, it seemed, as more than one pair of eyes was still fixed on her. It was hard to tell, though, what normal volume was with her eardrums about to rupture.

She rolled her eyes in the face of their disapproval. As if none of *them* had ever had to deal with a hungry baby. Smiling, she looked down at Rosie, determined to stay cheerful in the face of her cries. She was still cooing at her when she realised that Nic had left their table, and she only had a moment to wonder where he was before he emerged through the double doors with a steaming jug of water and the bottle.

What a hero. She could kiss him.

Well, actually, that pretty much felt like her default setting these days. But she was more grateful than ever to have him in her life right at that second. She watched him walk towards her as if he were carrying the Holy Grail.

'One bottle,' he declared as he closed the door to the deck behind him and passed it over to her.

She'd expected him to be sprinting back through the doors as soon as he'd offloaded his cargo, but instead he dropped down onto a bench, spreading his arms across the back. Lily sat beside him as Rosie started sucking on the bottle, quiet at last.

'Why don't you go in and eat?' she said to him. 'It seems a shame for us both to be missing out on lunch.'

'I don't mind—'

'Honestly—go and eat. She's perfectly happy now, so I'll be back in soon.'

He hesitated for a second, but then stood and headed for the door. Lily leaned back against the bench and closed her eyes for a moment, letting herself drift with the rhythmic rocking of the boat. At the sound of the deck doors opening her eyes flew open—to see Nic juggling glasses and plates as he fought to shut the door behind him.

'If Rosie's picnicking out here, seems only fair that we get to as well,' he said with a grin.

Lily risked a glance into the dining room and could see that more than one set of eyes was disapprovingly set in their direction.

'Open up.'

A forkful of delicate tartlet appeared in front of her nose and Lily hesitated, meeting Nic's eyes as he offered the food to her. *Definitely* too intimate for friends. But Rosie's weight in her arms reminded her that this wasn't romance, it was practicality, and she opened her mouth, let her lips close around the cold tines of the fork.

Closing her eyes seemed too decadent, too sensuous. But holding Nic's gaze as he fed her so intimately seemed like a greater danger. As balsamic vinegar hit her palate she smiled. With food this good, why let herself be distracted by anything else?

She sat looking out across the water, enjoying seeing the city that was so familiar to her with the unfamiliar smells and sounds of the boat. Nic's arm was still stretched across the back of the bench, but she didn't move away. It was too easy, too comfortable to sit like this, enjoying the moments of quiet and savouring their lunch.

Eventually, when both plates were cleared and Rosie had finished her formula, Nic nodded towards the dining room.

'Think we can risk human company again?'

CHAPTER NINE

NIC LOOKED DOWN at Rosie, milk-drunk and sleepy again.

'I think we should be safe,' Lily said, setting the bottle down beside them, lifting Rosie to her shoulder and starting to rub her back.

'Let me do that,' Nic offered, already reaching for Rosie.

He hadn't meant to: he'd been clear with himself that the only way he could let himself explore this connection with Lily was if he remembered to keep his distance with Rosie. But he could hardly invite them out for the day and not expect to help. It was what any friend would do, he told himself. Friendship wasn't just offering the parts of yourself that were easy. Taking the parts of the other person that fitted with your life. It meant taking the hard bits too, exposing yourself to hurt, trusting that the other person was looking out for you.

They'd agreed that a relationship was too much to take on, but if they were going to be friends he was going to be a *good* friend.

He nestled the baby on his shoulder as they walked back inside, and for a moment he was caught by her new baby smell—a scent that threw him back ten years, to the happiest and hardest moments of his life. His eyes closed and his steps faltered for a second, but he forced himself forward, pushing through the pain of his past and reminding himself that Rosie wasn't Max, and Lily wasn't Clare.

As they reached the table their main courses arrived, and he slid into his seat with Rosie still happy on his shoulder.

'This looks amazing,' declared Lily, looking down at the plates of perfectly pink lamb and buttery potatoes. She reached for her knife and fork, but then hesitated. 'Are you sure you don't want me to take her?'

'You can if you want,' Nic told her, wary of overstepping some line. 'But I don't mind.'

Lily's eyes dropped to Rosie again as she thought for a minute.

'No, you're right. It would be silly to disturb her when she's settled.'

He picked up his fork, wondering how he was meant to tackle a rack of lamb one-handed.

'Here,' Lily said, with a smile and a sparkle in her eye. She pinned the meat with a fork while he cut it, and when she caught the maître d's shocked expression, she laughed out loud. 'I don't think I've ever caused such a scandal before,' she whispered to him.

He laughed in return, relieved to feel the tension leaching from the air.

'I feel like we're doing him a service. His life must have been very sheltered if we're so shocking to him. Maybe we should up the ante? Give him something to really disapprove of…?'

Oh, did he like the sound of *that*. His skin prickled,

his grin widened and he leaned closer across the table. 'What exactly did you have in mind?'

Lily blushed.

God, it was such a turn-on when she did that—when the evidence of her desire chased across her skin like watercolours on a damp page.

'I…I…I don't think I really thought that sentence through,' she said at last with a coy smile.

He laughed again, feeling his shoulders relax, leaning back in his chair as they seemed to find common ground again…as he started to feel the subtle pull and heat between them that had brought them together in the first place.

'Maybe I'll ask you again another time,' he suggested, unable to resist this spark between them. 'When we've a little more privacy and a little less company.'

She looked up at him from under her lashes—a look, he suspected, not entirely uncalculated.

'Maybe I'll give it a little thought this afternoon.'

For a moment the silence spanned warm and comfortable between them, and he held her gaze as gently and sensuously as if he was reaching out and touching her.

A little choking sound from the baby he'd almost forgotten was in his arms drew his attention and he smiled down at her, so exposed from the conversation with Lily that he didn't have a moment to try and defend himself, had no chance of raising any sort of resistance to those adorably round cheeks or her big blue eyes.

'Sorry, little Rosie,' he told her, mopping her up automatically and shifting her to his other shoulder. 'I guess we weren't paying you enough attention.'

Lily gave him a complicated smile, but then with one more bite of potato she dropped her knife and fork.

'That was incredible—truly,' she told him. 'The closest thing to heaven I've ever eaten.'

'Agreed,' he said, looking a little longingly at the lamb still on his plate.

'I'll take her back,' Lily told him, her tone brooking no argument this time. 'Seriously—you'll kick yourself if you don't eat every bite.'

CHAPTER TEN

THE BOAT SLOWED as they approached the wharf and Lily could practically feel the collective sigh of relief from everyone on board. Not that she cared. The three of them had enjoyed another picnic out on deck, when Rosie had been testy again during dessert, and she couldn't help but think that it had been nicer, anyway, to be out in the fresh air than in that dining room, with its candles that spoke of a romance they were definitely *not* going to be pursuing.

Part of her had wanted to explain to the other diners —to confess that she'd thought more than once that maybe if she was Rosie's real mum she might be better at this. She might be flailing a little less at the prospect of a baby whose needs were really pretty simple if only she could work out the code that everyone else seemed to understand. She couldn't really blame them for being annoyed. No doubt they'd paid handsomely for their lunch, and hadn't expected to encounter a crying baby while they enjoyed it. But their silent judgement was cutting nonetheless.

At least she'd had a partner in crime.

Nic had actually taken the baby today. Offered to help and then cooed at her and rocked her until she was calm. Though the ghost of pain and doubt etched into his every feature was enough to show her that, romantic as the setting was, his thoughts were anything but. There was nothing more likely to put him off, she thought, than being reminded of the realities of parenting.

'You okay there?' Nic asked, breaking into her reverie. 'You look a million miles away.'

The car had met them as they'd disembarked and they were crawling through London traffic again, on their way to sightseeing event number two.

The car stopped outside the Tower of London, and she sent Nic a questioning glance. She couldn't hide her deep breath of apprehension. The last time she'd been to the Tower had been years ago, and she'd had to fight her way through crowds, elbow her way into a picnic spot and strain her ears to hear the commentary from the obligatory Beefeater. She couldn't imagine it being any more relaxing with Rosie strapped to her chest.

'We're here,' Nic announced with a smile.

He reached for her hand to help her out of the car, and then reached in after her to take Rosie from her seat. He handed the baby straight over, but she couldn't help seeing a tiny bit of progress.

They were met at the gate by a uniformed Beefeater, and as she passed through the entrance she realised how different it felt from the last time she'd been there. Looking around her, she realised why. The place was deserted. How on earth had he pulled *this* off?

The Beefeater puffed up his chest as he turned round and launched into a clearly well-practised speech, welcoming them to Her Majesty's Royal Palace and Fortress, The Tower of London. 'There's a thousand years

of history here, sir, madam: more than you could dis-
cover in a week. So what would you like to see? The
armouries? The torture display? The Crown Jewels?'

Lily gave an involuntary gasp at the mention of the
jewels. The day of her teenaged visit the Jewel House
had been packed and sweaty. She'd managed to get
stuck behind someone with a huge backpack on the
moving conveyor, and had passed through without getting one decent look at a crown.

She looked up at Nic, who laughed. 'Looks like the
Crown Jewels it is,' he declared to their Yeoman Guard.

'You're sure you don't mind? I'd understand if diamonds weren't your thing.'

'That look on your face is exactly my thing,' he told
her quietly as their guide discreetly moved away. 'And
if it's a diamond that gets it there...'

His sentence trailed into silence, but his gaze never
faltered from hers. He *was* talking about diamonds?
Had he realised what he'd said? Of course he didn't
mean a *diamond* diamond—the type that led you up
the aisle and towards happy-ever-after. But if he'd
meant nothing by it, why wasn't he looking away.
Why was he reaching out and touching her face, as if
trying to see something, touch something, that wasn't
quite there?

His hand dropped gently to cup the back of Rosie's
head, then lower still to Lily's waist, pulling her towards him. She closed her eyes as he leaned in for a
kiss, and felt the lightest, gentlest brush of lips over
hers. For a moment she couldn't move. Not even to kiss
him back or push him away. In that moment she didn't
know which she wanted more—which she was more
scared of. Because this kiss was something different.

It wasn't the desperate press of his lips on hers at the hospital, or that regretfully friendly kiss on the cheek. This kiss was the start of something new. Something more than they'd had before…something more serious…something more frightening.

Rosie let out a squawk, clearly less than impressed at being trapped between the two of them, and Nic backed off a little, his smile more of a slow-burning candle than a full-beam sun.

He called over to their guide and let him know that they were ready.

Rosie started to whimper a little as they headed over to the Jewel House, and their guide slowed a little.

'Aw, is she out of sorts? She looks just the same age as my granddaughter—and that girl has a pair of lungs on her, I can tell you. Do you want to sit somewhere quiet with her for a while?'

'Thank you, but she's just tired. I think if we keep walking she'll send herself off.'

'Of course. Mum knows best,' he told her with a wink. 'Though if you ask me…' he gave her a careful look '…it's probably Dad's turn.'

He carried on speaking, but Lily couldn't make out what he was saying. Her focus was pinned entirely on Nic as his face fell, then paled, and then as he slowly put himself back together. His eyes refocused, and his jaw returned to its usual position.

'Here,' he said, just as Lily caught something about Colonel Blood in 1671 from their guide. 'He's right. My turn.'

He held his hands out for her, and Lily sent him the clearest *Are you sure?* look she could manage without speaking out loud. He took Rosie in his arms and lifted her to his chin, then leaned down and pressed a kiss to the top of her head. He closed his eyes for a moment and Lily knew that he was remembering. But then he looked up at her with a brave smile, grabbed her hand and squeezed.

They followed the guard, and she tried to listen to his stories, tried to take in the information, but really she just wanted to look. And not at the diamonds or the gold or the ancient artefacts. She wanted to watch Nic with Rosie. Wanted to witness the way he was resisting his hurt and his past and trying to endure, trying to move on. And he was doing it for her.

When they emerged from the Jewel House the evening was starting to draw in. Car headlights were lighting up Tower Bridge, and the banks of the river were bustling with tourists calling it a day mixed with commuters heading home.

'A walk along the river before we head home?' Nic asked. 'I had thought maybe dinner, but…'

Lily burst out laughing, remembering how they'd spent barely half an hour of their lunch actually in the dining room. With a few hours' distance suddenly the whole cruise seemed like a farce. For dinner she wanted nothing more than a sofa and a cheese sandwich. Michelin-starred cuisine was all well and good, but you couldn't exactly eat it in your pyjamas. Or with a baby nearby, apparently.

'I think we'd better quit while we're ahead,' she said. 'Lunch was spectacular, in so many ways, but I think Rosie needs her bed. Enough excitement for her for one day.'

'I understand. We should probably head back.'

Lily nodded, suddenly feeling sombre. The prospect

of an evening together in the apartment was suddenly overwhelming. That kiss—there'd be nowhere to hide from it once they got home.

In the privacy and seclusion of the car, nipping through London traffic, Lily's thoughts were heading in one direction and one direction only—behind the so far firmly shut door of her bedroom. She risked a glance up at Nic, wondering whether her feelings were showing on her face. Were they going to talk about this again? Put aside all their good intentions to do the sensible thing? That kiss had promised so much that couldn't be unsaid.

But she stayed silent—as did Nic. Silent in the car, silent in the lift, silent until Rosie was settled in her cot and they were alone in the living room—with nothing and no one standing between them and the conversation they were avoiding.

Nic let out a long, slow breath, rubbing his hand across the back of his neck, and for a minute Lily wondered if she'd completely misread what had been going on between them—maybe he was happy with things as they were? Maybe he was only interested in being friends?

She risked a glance up at him and all her doubts fled. The heat in his eyes told her everything she needed to know about how he felt—and it was a lot more than friendly. She felt that heat travel to the depths of her belly, warming her from the inside until it reached her face as a smile. He pulled gently on her hand, bringing her close to him, and planted his other hand on her hip.

'Is this a good idea?' she asked, knowing the answer…knowing just as well that it wasn't going to stop them.

'Terrible,' Nic answered, dropping her hand and finding her cheek with his palm. 'Want to stop?'

It took considerable effort not to laugh in his face. Stop? How *could* they stop? They'd tried to avoid this. They'd talked about exactly why this was a bad idea. Looking deep into Nic's eyes, she could see that he still had reservations, that he still didn't fully believe this was the right thing to do. But stop...?

'No.'

'Everything we said, Lily—it still stands. I've not changed who I am, what happened...'

'I know. But what are we meant to do—just ignore this? I can't, Nic. It feels too...big. Too important. So let's see where it goes. No guarantees. No promises. Let's just stop fight—'

His lips captured hers before the word was even out, and she knew that they were lost. They'd been crazy to think that they could live here, together, and pretend that this wasn't happening—that their bodies hadn't been dragging them towards each other, however unwillingly, since the moment that they'd met.

With her spine wedged against a console table and her feet barely on the floor, Lily thought how easy it would be to surrender completely. To let Nic literally sweep her off her feet, caveman-style if he wanted, and really see where they could take this.

But as his hands found the sensitive skin at the back of her knees, lifting her until her legs wrapped around his waist, she knew that the easy road wasn't the right one.

'Nic...' she gasped into his ear, not able to articulate more than that one syllable.

But he'd perched her gently on the table and now, al-

though his breathing was still ragged, he pulled back—
just an inch…just enough to give her the space she
needed to clear her head. His expression held all his
questions without him having to say a word.

'Slower,' Lily said eventually, when she'd regained
the power of speech. 'That was…I want to see where
this will go, but…slower. Slower than that.'

She could barely believe that she'd managed to get
the words out, and even as she was saying them she
was already half regretting that she wasn't more fear-
less. But she couldn't be. Just because they had decided
to stop fighting, it didn't mean that she had decided
to be stupid. There was no happy ending in sight—no
easy way to set aside everything they'd convinced each
other was good reason to stay apart.

They'd still have to work through it…whatever it
was that made Nic's eyes dim at the most unexpected
times. It wasn't all going to disappear because they
wanted things to be easy. And until they were more
sure of each other there was only so far she could take
this.

CHAPTER ELEVEN

SUNDAY MORNING, LILY WOKE to sunshine at the curtains and Rosie gurgling happily in her crib. She stared at the wall opposite, trying to picture Nic just on the other side of it, sprawled across the king-size bed she'd seen when she'd sneaked a look at his room. And she could be in there with him now, she thought, rather than be trying to conjure the feeling of his arms around her waist, the warmth of his chest warming her back as she turned on the pillow and drifted back to sleep...

If only she hadn't been so darned sensible last night.

Much as she was cursing herself, she was glad, really, that she'd made the decision she had. Sure, daybreak wrapped in Nic sounded like perfection—but then what about breakfast? Lunch? All the conversations they hadn't had yet? The things that needed to be said before they decided if whatever it was between them could turn from 'let's see where this goes' into something more real, more lasting?

Footsteps padded down the hallway, and as they approached her room she held her breath, wondering whether they would stop—whether Nic wanted to pick up where they'd left that kiss last night. But they faded again, towards the front door, until she heard a key turn in the lock and then silence.

He'd just gone! Without a word! A cold shiver traced her spine. But she forced herself out of bed and into the kitchen, determined not to read too much into it. He often went for a run at this time of day, before the streets were busy. But it was a Sunday—and, more than that, it was the morning after *that* kiss, when she had a million things to say and no idea where to start. Was that what he was avoiding?

She shook her head as she boiled the kettle and scooped formula. Who said he was avoiding anything?

When he strolled into the apartment at half past ten, still in his running gear, she'd just got Rosie down for a sleep and was thinking of following her back to bed. But the sight of Nic's legs in his scantily cut running shorts gave her second thoughts.

'Good run?' she asked, having still not entirely shaken the worry that he'd left early that morning to avoid her. But he was smiling—beaming, actually— as he fiddled with the coffee machine.

'Brilliant—really good. What about you? Good morning?'

'Milk, nappies, sleep. Pretty much standard.' She said it with a smile, and she could hear the dreamy edge in her voice. It might be hard work, but she would be hard pressed to think of another job that was more worth it.

'I stopped by the office,' Nic said as he placed a cup of coffee in front of her. 'Had a bit of a brainwave when I was running…'

Lily's eyebrows drew together.

'What sort of idea?'

'What have you got planned this week?'

She gave it a moment's thought. One tiny design job that she had to finish and email to her client, and other than that more milk, more nappies, more sleep.

'Just the usual.'

'Then come to Rome with me.'

He was still talking, but a crash of thoughts drowned out his words as she tried to process what he'd just said. A trip to Rome with the man she knew she was rapidly falling for? How could she say no? *Why* would she say no?

Nic squeezed her hand.

'Lily? Still with me?'

'I am—sorry. I think that's an incredible idea, but...'

Even as she was saying the words the real world began to intrude.

'But you're worried about the practicalities and about Rosie? I know—of course you are. But she'll have everything she needs. The logistics might not be easy, but they're not impossible.'

'She doesn't even have a passport.'

'No, but she does have an appointment at the passport office tomorrow. *If* you decide it's what you want,' he hastened to add. 'There'd be a skycot on the flight, and a cot in your room at the hotel. Formula, nappies... I've organised a pram and a car seat—the same ones as you have here—to use while we're there. I think I've thought of everything—if not the hotel's concierge is on standby for anything baby-related. We can even organise a nanny, if you want one.'

Lily slumped back in her chair, her mouth agape.

'I don't know what to say.'

'Say *yes*,' Nic said with a boyish eagerness. 'Have you been to Italy before?'

'No, I've never been to Italy...' she said, her words coming out slowly as her brain fought to catch up. 'But I'm not sure that really comes into my decision. I've got to think practically.'

'You can think practically if you want, but I swear it's all taken care of. Instead you could think about Rome: sipping coffee in a quiet *piazza*, genuine Italian cuisine, the shopping...'

'You're a great salesman—very persuasive. No wonder you were head-hunted.'

'What can I say? I'm only human. Now, stop changing the subject. If you need time to think about it, that's fine.'

Would she use the time to think about it? Or would she use it to talk herself out of it? *Rome*. It was hardly the sort of opportunity that came along every day. And the opportunity to take a spur-of-the-moment trip to a romantic city with Nic seemed like a once-in-a-lifetime sort of thing. She'd be mad to say no.

'Okay, yes. I'd love to.' She could feel the smile spreading across her cheeks, feel the warmth in the pit of her stomach rising to glow in her chest and her heart. '*Rome*, Nic. I don't know where to start being excited about that!'

Nic simply sat and watched as Lily enthused about Rome, so pleased that he'd been able to convince her to come with him. He'd had a flash of inspiration this morning and not been able to rest until he'd got the details in place. His trip had been booked for a while—a meeting with a fabric supplier he'd been in contact with several times over the years. And now that he and Lily had decided to see where this chemistry between them might go, Rome seemed like too good an opportunity to miss.

For a brief moment—just a split second—he'd been tempted to call his sister and ask if she'd babysit Rosie for a night. But he'd stopped himself. He wanted Lily and everything that came with her. He couldn't pretend—didn't want to pretend—that Rosie wasn't going to be a part of their life together. He'd made a few calls, pulled in a few favours, and had plans for the trip underway before he'd even got to the office.

'You know, you don't talk about your family much,' he remarked, once they'd exhausted all possible Roman topics of conversation.

'There's not a lot to tell,' Lily said with a shrug, but the shadow that darkened her eyes told him a different story.

'I know how sad it makes you that you and your sister aren't close…'

He wasn't sure why he was pushing the issue. Maybe it was because he wanted to be close to her, to *really* know her. He'd laid bare the darkest parts of his own history, but he knew so little about her. How could they try and be something more than friends to one another if he didn't really know her?

'It does,' she admitted. 'But maybe now… Maybe things will be better.'

'Was there a big falling-out?'

Lily shook her head as she drank her coffee. A drop caught on her lower lip and he watched, entranced, as her tongue sneaked out to rescue it.

'Nothing dramatic.'

'How do your parents feel about it?'

She caught her breath in a gasp, and though she tried to cover it he knew that he'd just stumbled into dangerous waters.

'Actually, my parents aren't around. My dad never was, and my mum died when I was twelve.'

He felt a gut-wrenching stab of pain on her behalf, and at the same time wanted to kick himself for causing her distress. What an idiot he was to go stumbling around in her past. If she'd wanted to talk about her family she would have brought it up. But then he was sure he'd heard Kate say something about her visiting her family. If not her sister or her parents, then who?

'I'm sorry, Lily. I didn't mean to pry. We don't have to—'

'It's fine,' she told him, settling her mug on the table. 'I don't mind talking about her. It's nice, actually, to have a reminder occasionally.'

'What was she like?'

'She was lovely—and amazing. That doesn't seem like enough, but I'm not sure how else…' Her voice trailed off and she rested her chin on her hand, leaning on the table. 'It was all rather wonderful when I was growing up—which, knowing what I do now about what it is to bring up a child on your own…'

She still had no idea how her mother had done it. Every day she spent battling to keep her head above water with Rosie was another day when her respect for her mother grew exponentially. And when she found herself looking at her own efforts and wondering why she found it so hard…

'And I had a big sister to look out for me. But then Mum was in a car accident and everything changed.'

'I'm so sorry.'

He couldn't believe that he hadn't known this about her before now. That she'd let him talk about his loss and his grief while never hinting that there were people she loved missing from her own life.

'It's not as bad as all that,' she said, catching his eye and giving a little smile. 'At the time, obviously, it was horrendous. But I was placed with a wonderful foster family who helped me come to terms with losing my mother. Helped me so that I could remember her with love, remember the wonderful family that we were. I was lucky to find a second set of people to love me and take care of me.'

He marvelled at her composure, but sensed that her sister's story was somewhat different.

'And Helen?'

'Helen's older,' she said. 'She was sixteen when we lost Mum—too old for foster care. Not that that was what she wanted anyway. After Mum was gone it was like she wanted to prove that she didn't need her. She wanted to do her own thing, take care of herself. She was always welcome with my foster family, and we all tried hard to make her feel included, but it wasn't what she wanted. With our mum gone, the "half" part of being her half-sister suddenly seemed to matter more than ever.'

There were only so many times that he could say he was sorry before it started to sound trite. He couldn't fathom the way Lily had dealt with these blows—how she had come out the other side able to smile fondly when she thought about the family she'd once belonged to but which had since fallen apart. When he'd lost his son and then his fiancée, it had been as if the world had changed overnight. As if the warmth of the sun had stopped reaching him. He'd stopped living. Whereas Lily had grieved and then moved on.

'You didn't stay in touch?'

'We tried. *I* tried. I'd write to her—letters at first, then emails. Sometimes she'd reply and sometimes not. Eventually my letters started coming back to me and the emails started bouncing. She'd drop me a line occasionally, but the message was pretty clear. She was happier without me in her life—I think I was a reminder of what she'd lost.'

'But when she was really in trouble it was you she came to. She must trust you—love you—a lot.'

'I've thought about that. A lot, actually. And done a little bit of reading. I'm not sure that was why she left Rosie with me. Perhaps it was just because we're related. Maybe she didn't want Rosie in the care system. Hadn't completely decided what she wanted for her. Perhaps she thought that if she left her with me and changed her mind she could get her back. It didn't matter *who* I was—it only mattered that we had the same mother.'

'Oh, Lily.' He reached for her hand, turned it under his and threaded their fingers together. 'I can't believe that's true. I think she knows just what a special person you are—that you'll take care of her daughter without even questioning it. That you'll give her the happy childhood Helen remembers having.'

'Perhaps…'

Lily smiled, though he could see that there were tears gathering in her eyes.

'So, what's happening with…?' He wasn't sure what to call it. The Rosie Situation? 'With your guardianship? Have you had any update from the social worker?'

Lily explained the situation—that it was looking more and more likely that she would become Rosie's permanent guardian—and he tried hard to pin down how he felt. Tried to judge the proportions of fear, trepidation, excitement and affection that seemed constantly to battle for supremacy in his heart.

He wasn't sure that he could admit it to Lily, but maybe he could admit it to himself. In those early days, when he'd first been getting to know her, despite her fierce protection of Rosie, he'd managed to convince himself that her guardianship would only be temporary. That he could let himself fantasise because one day Rosie's mother would return, Lily would be a simple aunt again, and the baby's presence in her life would fade to the background. Then there would be nothing to come between him and Lily.

Now he knew that wasn't going to be the case. And it was too late—way too late—to stop falling for her. But what would happen when he hit the ground? He tried to imagine that life and it still filled him with a cold dread. He wanted to embrace all the possibilities that a relationship with Lily might bring, but when he allowed himself to think about the certainties of it he was filled with fear.

He watched her across the table and saw how she became shy under his gaze, dipping her eyes and concentrating far more than she needed to on sipping her coffee. She still wasn't sure of him—and with good reason. She deserved a lover who had no reservations, who was ready for a commitment to her, and he wasn't sure that was him—not yet.

For the first time he questioned whether he'd done the right thing in inviting her to Rome, whether that was leading her on—but, no. Rome was different. It was a way for them to get to know each other better, not a promise.

Three days to plan and she was just thinking about waxing her legs *now*? She glanced at her watch. Not a hope. Nic would be back from work in half an hour, her hair was still wet, and dinner was at least an hour off going in the oven. In fact most of it was still in the supermarket. Rosie was overdue a bath and it was veering dangerously close to being past her bedtime.

Where had three days gone? And how was it that she found it so impossible to do something as simple as cook dinner? Since the moment Rosie had turned up all she'd wanted to do was be a good mum…aunt… sister. To make a family for Rosie and for herself. But it seemed as if every time she thought she had it sorted she found herself in the middle of a disaster of her own making. They sneaked up on her and were suddenly right in front of her eyes.

She heard his key in the lock just as she had Rosie stripped off and ready for her bath. Cursing his bad timing, she wrapped the baby in a towel and carried her with her as she went to the door. Her plan had been to have an uninterrupted bedtime routine for Rosie this evening—to have her down and sleeping before Nic got home, so they could enjoy dinner together before heading off on their trip first thing tomorrow. But Rosie had slept late this afternoon. So she'd fed late and played late. And now—almost—she was being bathed late.

And then Nic was there, and in a moment her stress fell away. The width of his smile created fine lines of pleasure around his eyes as he leaned in to kiss her without hesitation.

'Hi,' she breathed, letting her eyes shut and enjoying that simple pleasure.

When she opened them she realised that the man was not only absurdly good-looking and radiating charm, he was also brandishing carrier bags and a bottle of red wine. It was almost enough to have her crying into Rosie's towel.

'I've interrupted bathtime,' he said, pointing out the obvious. 'I thought I'd leave a bit early and make a start on dinner. Couldn't wait to get home to you, actually, kick off our holiday tonight instead of in the morning.'

There were no games, no subtexts.

'You ladies get back to it, and I'll have dinner ready when you're done.'

Lily opened her mouth to argue: she'd promised him dinner and wine on the table when he got home—a small way of thanking him for the holiday.

'You're a hero,' she told him, meeting his honesty with her own. 'A genuine, real-life hero. Are you sure you don't mind?'

'My pleasure,' he said, already opening drawers and cupboards and emptying the carrier bags onto the worktop.

She shut the bathroom door behind her and checked the temperature of the water, smiling to herself when she found it was still warm enough—no time wasted there. She slid Rosie into the bath and soaped her, distracting her with bubbles as she washed her hair and ran a flannel over her face, rubbing away the last few remnants of milk.

And as she went through their bathtime routine her mind strayed to the man in the kitchen, wondering what his expectations were for this evening…wondering how well prepared he had come. Had he replayed their conversations as often as she had? Had he wondered when would be the right time to take their relationship further? When 'slow' would become impossible?

And what would that next step mean?

Of course she was hoping that they would make love, but doing something like that didn't come without strings attached for Lily. For her it would be a commitment—but did Nic feel the same?

She left the bathroom with Rosie all clean and fresh and tucked into her pyjamas, wishing that she looked half as good herself. Unfortunately she knew that she looked little less than crazed. And, while she couldn't *see* any stains on her T-shirt, the laws of parenting probability meant that there had to be one there somewhere.

When she reached the kitchen Nic was cooking up a storm, but everything seemed to be perfectly under control. What did *that* feel like? She tried to remember a time when her life had felt like her own, when she had been confident that she knew exactly what she was doing and that she was doing a good job. Some time in the haze her pre-Rosie life had become, she assumed.

The paradox plagued her. It was the time when she most wanted to pull her family together, to prove that she could be mother and sister and aunt with the best of them, and it all seemed entirely out of her hands. The more she fought to show that she could do this—

be the matriarch, hold it all together—the faster things spun around her.

Nic stopped stirring the sauce on the hob for long enough to steal a quick kiss, and Lily plonked herself on a stool at the breakfast bar, watching him for a moment.

The kettle clicked and she noticed the bottle and tin of formula standing next to it, ready to be made up.

'I figured if the grown-ups are hungry then Rosie might well be too,' he said.

He'd dropped the wooden spoon and now stood leaning against the counter, hands in pockets. Lily looked at him closely, observing the slight change in his posture, the tension that had sneaked into his body and was holding him a little stiffer. Still trying, still struggling, she deduced. But he kept coming back for more. Not only that, he'd come carrying dinner and was helping to make bottles. She couldn't judge him for still finding things hard: he had earned her respect for trying despite that.

'So, what's for dinner?' Lily asked, placing Rosie in her bouncy chair and making up the bottle.

'Not very exciting, I'm afraid. Gnocchi, pancetta, cream sauce, a bit of salad—I've brought a little of Italy home with me.'

'You are the consummate domestic goddess,' she told him with a smile, hoping that it would cover the twinge of—what? Resentment that that had been *her* role, *her* talent, until she was faced with her first real challenge?

He must see how much she was struggling. Must have guessed that she wouldn't be able to put dinner on the table for him. Not that she was even *trying* for

Stepford-wife-style Cordon Bleu cuisine. She'd have settled for managing to get oven chips ready.

Something of her fears must have shown on her face, because Nic pushed himself up from the counter, hands no longer in his pockets. Instead they were reaching for her waist and pulling her into him. Suddenly emotional, Lily kept her eyes lowered, not wanting to look up and show him how upset she was that she was *still* not getting this right.

'I'm sorry if I did the wrong thing,' he said. 'I only wanted us to have a nice relaxed night. I've been looking forward to this, and the last thing I wanted was to cause you more work, more stress.'

He palmed her cheek and she turned into the warmth of his skin instinctively, and then slowly looked up.

'It wasn't a criticism, or a judgement.' He leaned in further, and pressed a quick kiss to her lips. 'You're doing an amazing job with Rosie, and I just wanted to do my bit.'

Another kiss and her limbs started to feel loose and languid, her body like a gel that wanted to mould to him.

Nic pulled away slightly and rested his forehead on hers. 'I've been thinking about that all day. *Every* day, actually,' he admitted. 'The least you can do after keeping me awake three nights in a row is let me make you dinner.'

She smiled. He was good—she'd give him that.

'Thank you,' she said. 'It's a lovely thought. And, for the record, I *might* have thought about you too. Just once or twice.'

He broke into a grin at that, and swooped a kiss onto her cheek.

True to his word, once Rosie was in bed Nic set two places at the dining table, lit the candles, served Lily an enormous portion of gnocchi and filled up their wine glasses.

'This is incredible,' Lily said as she sat down.

'I wouldn't get carried away,' Nic told her with a self-effacing smile. 'It's just gnocchi and sauce.'

'It's gnocchi, sauce, good wine and better company. It's like being in an alien land, and it's divine.'

'Well, I can drink to that,' Nic said, raising his glass in a toast and clinking it against hers. 'So, what have I missed?'

He'd been in the office until late the last couple of nights, making sure that everything was in place for his trip.

'Well, I have two big pieces of news—Rosie lifted her head for the first time today, and then I thought she smiled at me…but it turned out to be gas. It's been hectic!' She laughed, wondering what he'd make of her day.

'I'm sure it *was* a smile,' Nic said. 'Most likely because she's got such a wonderful aunt to take care of her.'

Lily smiled, bashful, acknowledging his praise with a blush, if not his knowledge of development milestones.

'And did you get the work done that you needed to?' Nic asked.

'Only just,' Lily admitted. 'But it's done now. I've not got anything else lined up for the next few weeks so I can concentrate on Rosie. I'm sure I'll miss it soon enough, and want something to challenge me. A *different* sort of challenge,' she clarified, just in case he'd missed the point that Rosie was an Olympic-sized challenge in herself. 'I'm only going to take on small commissions for now, but it's good to keep my eye in… keep my skills ticking over.'

'I'm impressed,' Nic told her.

Lily shrugged off the compliment.

'No, seriously.' He reached out for her hand as she tried again to brush off his words. 'I'm actually in awe—I can't even think how you find time in the day for it all.'

Lily laughed. 'Oh, it's easy. You just forget the laundry, and mopping the floor, and filing your nails, and…'

'And focus on what's important. Like I said, you're incredible.'

Lily held her hands up and shook her head. 'Okay, that's officially as much as I can take. We're going to have to change the subject or I'll become unbearable. What about you? Did you get everything sorted that you needed to?'

'Everything's taken care of. All we have to do to-morrow is get in the car when it shows up.'

And then make some pretty huge decisions about their future.

That bit didn't need saying, but after the careful way they'd spent the last few days she thought they both knew that that was what Rome was really going to be about. About finding out what they wanted to be to each other. What risks they were prepared to take and what hopes they were going to nurture.

They lingered over their coffee, neither of them making a move to go to bed—alone or otherwise.

But as Lily stifled a yawn Nic stood and cleared

away the last few dishes. 'You look done in,' he said over his shoulder. 'And I'm ready to turn in. I guess we should call it a night.'

So he wasn't going to suggest it. Well, she shouldn't be surprised. She was the one who had insisted on 'slower' the last time things had got out of hand. The ball was really in her court now.

'If you're sure...' Lily said, aiming the lilt in her voice at pure temptation.

But he didn't look as if he was wavering.

'We've an early start tomorrow,' he said, but the tense lines of his forehead told her he was struggling to do the noble thing. 'It's probably best if we call it a night.'

'Of course.' Lily stood up, but the slight shake of her legs revealed her hidden emotions.

Nic stood too, and rested his hands lightly on her waist. 'It's not just that...' he told her.

He surprised her with his sudden honesty. But she supposed they *were* trying to see if they had any hope of a future together. If they couldn't talk to each other, be honest with each other now, at the outset, then what hope did they have?

'Don't think for a second that it's because I don't want to take you to bed—that I haven't been imagining it every day.' He was rewarded with a flash of colour in her cheeks, and he traced the colour with his fingertips and then his lips. 'But once we take that step I'm yours, Lily. Everything I am will belong to you. We both have a lot to think about...a lot to decide... Let's not rush. We have as much time as we want and as we need.'

She nodded, the smile on her lips now genuine, if a little wary.

He walked her to her bedroom door and grabbed her hands as she reached for the handle. 'Still time to say a proper goodnight,' he said, pulling her close and running the backs of his fingers down the soft skin of her arm. From there he rested his hands on her waist, until there was nothing between them but their heavy breaths.

He dipped his head and brushed his lips gently against hers, testing. But she smiled against him, yielding to him for a moment and then drawing back, yielding and drawing back—until one of his hands was at the nape of her neck, the other was clamped at her waist, and he was backing her slowly against the hard wood of the door. He was desperate for more, to feel her giving herself wholly to him. For her to stop her teasing and give him everything she was…to demand all of him in return.

When she opened her mouth to him and touched his tongue with hers he let out a low groan, his hand fisting behind her back. He leaned back and smiled at her flushed face, laughed a little breathily.

'Oh, you're good,' he said. 'Really, *really* good. But I'll see you in the morning.'

She nodded, biting her lip.

'If you're sure…' she said, with a minxy little smile. 'I guess I'll see you then.'

'I've never been less sure about anything in my life,' he said, and his voice had a little gravel in it as he tried to pull her closer again.

But her hands had found his chest and were pushing

gently. 'No, I won't take advantage,' she said. Then, more seriously, 'You're right. I want us to be sure.'

He nodded, reason starting to return to him as the blood returned to his brain. 'So I'll see you in the morning?'

'I'll be waiting.'

CHAPTER TWELVE

LILY LIFTED THE delicate espresso cup to her lips and savoured the full, rich flavour as it touched her lips. Nic hadn't made it up to the hotel suite yet, but the smell had been so tempting she'd not been able to wait. There was a lot of that going on at the moment, she realised, still not sure what to make of Nic's decision last night to go to his own bed—alone.

It was gentlemanly of him, and deep down of course she knew that it had been the right decision. There was too much at stake, too many ways they could get hurt, for them to rush a decision like that. But… But nothing. The fact that she'd been desperate for him since the moment he'd left her last night shouldn't be a part of their decision-making process.

Well, if you were going to try and temper a girl's disappointment a suite in a five-star hotel in the Piazza di Spagna was a good start. She wandered around the living area of the suite now, stopping to admire the artwork adorning the walls and the artfully placed side tables. It was exquisite—unlike anywhere she'd seen before, never mind stayed. Rosie was still fast asleep in her carrycot, as she had been since they had left the airport. True to his word, Nic had arranged everything they needed, and they had been whisked from house to car to airport to hotel with barely a whimper from Rosie and barely any intervention from her.

There were two doors leading off the living area and she crossed to the one on her left, still a little awe-struck by her surroundings. She tried the handle to the door and found it unlocked. She nudged the door open, feeling as if she was about to be caught snooping. An enormous bed—king-size? Emperor? Bigger?—dom-inated the room, draped with rich silky curtains and topped with crisp white sheets. Her room? she won-dered. Or Nic's? Then she spotted the cot in the cor-ner and her question was answered. Her room. And Rosie's. For a moment she wished she'd wake, so that she could share her excitement with her, waltz her around the suite and wow her with all the finery she couldn't yet understand.

But she'd woken her early once before, and that hadn't exactly gone well. She took another sip of her coffee, wondering where Nic had got to. He'd wanted a quick word with the concierge—that was all he'd told her as he'd encouraged her to go straight up to the room. The coffee had been awaiting them, along with fruit and pastries. She'd intended to wait for Nic to arrive before she indulged further, but now she ques-tioned that decision. Well, if he was going to leave her here, he had only himself to blame.

She'd just selected the lightest pastry from the plat-ter when the door opened and she was caught red-handed.

'Glad to see you're settling in,' Nic said, tossing his carry-on bag onto the couch and crossing to the table to grab a pastry for himself. 'These are incredible,' he said, devouring the morsel in a few quick bites. 'Worth flying out for these alone.'

'The coffee's not bad,' Lily said, with a smile to show she was joking. 'And the room's just about adequate.'

He surprised her with a quick kiss to the lips.

'I'm glad you like it,' he said. 'I've not stayed here before, but I've heard great things.'

'Not your usual haunt?'

'No, I normally stay somewhere a little more…rustic. But I promised you girls an adventure in Rome, and I don't think that Nonna Lucia's *pensione* really fits the bill.'

'Nonna Lucia?'

'She looks after me when I'm here—seems to rather like having someone to fuss over.'

'Won't she be offended that we're not staying with her?'

'Actually, I already ran it by her. I knew she'd be offended if she found out somehow. I explained that I was bringing a friend with me, and that we'd need some more space, and she nodded in a very knowing way and said, "Of course." I think maybe I've given her the wrong idea…'

Lily laughed, delighted with this description. 'Will I get to meet her?'

'If you'd like to. I know that we'd be welcome any time. I was just speaking to the concierge about dinner, and he was making some enquiries, but if you'd rather—?'

She thought back to how well a fancy meal had gone last time and didn't hesitate. 'I'd love to. I'd like to see what your life is like when you're travelling,' she said. 'If it's not all five-star suites and divine coffee.'

'Oh, Nonna's coffee is second to none,' he reassured her. 'I'll call her to arrange tonight—if you're sure you don't want to go somewhere more...?'

'I'm sure,' she told him.

'Well, that's dinner sorted, then. What do you fancy doing in the meantime? Settle in here a little longer? Or head out for some sightseeing?'

She glanced around the room, caught sight of the bed in the other room, and suddenly lost her nerve. 'Let's go out,' she said. 'I don't want to waste a minute of this trip.'

'Brilliant,' Nic replied. 'What about Rosie? I don't want to wake her if she's not ready, but Rome's not known for being pushchair-friendly. There should be a baby carrier around here somewhere, though.'

Torn, Lily tried to decide what to do. She didn't want to wake the baby, and risk her grumping through the afternoon, but the whole of Rome was waiting for them and she couldn't wait to see it. She glanced at her watch, wondering how much longer she would sleep. Perhaps another half an hour...

'What about this?' Nic said. 'We head up to the roof terrace—I can carry the carrycot. We take in Rome from above, and once she wakes we hit the town.'

'Perfect.'

An hour later Rosie was awake, looking from Nic to Lily, wondering who was most likely to give her attention and a cuddle. Lily got to her first, reaching down to the carrycot, which Nic had tucked into a shady corner, and scooping Lily into her arms.

'What do you think she makes of it so far?' Nic asked.

Lily laughed. 'She's been asleep since we left the airport! But I'm sure she'll love it as much as I will.'

'Shall we dig out that baby carrier and find out?'

They wandered out from the hotel with Rosie strapped to Lily's front, and the heat of the summer afternoon hit them hard. The roof terrace had been shaded, with creeping plants over gazebos, but out on the street there was nothing more than her wide-brimmed hat to protect her and Rosie's pale skin from the burn of the sun.

'You okay?' Nic asked.

'I didn't realise how hot it is,' she told him, fanning her face. 'The terrace was so shady.'

'Let's keep off the main streets, then,' Nic said, taking her hand and leading her down one of the winding side streets that led off the main drag.

She breathed out a sigh of relief as they walked along in the shadow of the buildings, the blare of car horns and buzzing mopeds fading behind them.

'Better?' he asked.

'This is lovely.' She squeezed his hand as they passed a sleepy-looking restaurant, its owners still at their siesta, perhaps.

'So, what do you want to see? The Colosseum? The Vatican? Trevi Fountain? We can start wherever you like.'

'They all sound nice...' Lily started.

'But...?'

'But this is nice too,' she finished, smiling up at him as he pulled her to a stop.

The lane had meandered past delicious-smelling

bakeries and traditional-looking *trattorie* until it had become no more than a sun-dappled alleyway, with apartments on either side, their balconies spilling colour and texture as flowers hung down from the walls.

'Seeing Rome like this…it's something I never really imagined. But what I'm most looking forward to about this trip—' She bit her lip, looking for the confidence she needed to make this confession. Then she remembered his honesty the night before, and knew that she owed him nothing less than the truth. 'I want to spend it with *you*. Whether we do that at the Colosseum or here—and frankly this is the prettiest little street I've ever seen—doesn't seem that important.'

She watched him carefully, wondering what he had made of her words. The expression on his face left her none the wiser. Then, instead of speaking, he dropped his head and his lips landed on hers, soft and gentle. Their warmth, his taste, was becoming deliciously familiar. With each time they kissed she felt more comfortable, and that heat in her belly grew, leaving her wanting more and more. The backs of his fingers brushed the skin of her neck, her collarbone, and it was only as she instinctively moved closer that she remembered that Rosie was there between them—physically as well as emotionally.

With a smile, she pulled away. Nic met her gaze and held it for a few seconds, then, with his eyes on hers until the last minute, he dropped his head slowly and kissed Rosie on the top of her head.

He straightened, meeting Lily's eyes with an intense look. 'I want to make you promises, Lily. I want to tell you that I'll be everything you deserve. But I can't.'

Lily froze, not wanting to break the intensity of the moment, knowing that Nic had more to say.

'I've been here before, Lily. I've tried to be the family man, tried to support a partner and a family, and it didn't end well.'

'Nic, you can't blame yourself for what happened to Max.'

'If that was all I had to feel guilty about...' His voice was filled with anguish and his eyes were faraway, lost in the past. 'It wasn't just Max I let down, Lily. It was Clare. After what happened she needed me. Needed her fiancé to be there for her, to talk to her about what had just happened. To try and find a way to get past it. I couldn't do it.'

'Nic, everyone copes in different ways.'

'That's no excuse. She needed something from me—something very simple—and I couldn't give it to her. It was *my* fault that our relationship broke down after Max died. *My* fault that we fell apart when she thought she was already at rock bottom. You need to know this, Lily, before you decide where you want this to go. You need to know that if—God forbid—it all goes wrong, and you lose Rosie, I can't promise to be there for you. You deserve someone who can.'

Lily stood and stared at him for a moment, and shivered even in the thirty-degree heat. This was what he'd been hiding, then—this was the shadow she'd glimpsed and never understood.

'Nic, I can't believe that it was all your responsibility. I'm sure you tried your hardest.'

'You're right—I did,' he said, his voice steadier now. 'I tried my hardest and it wasn't enough. I like you—a hell of a lot. I don't want to keep fighting it. But if we're doing this you deserve to know what you're getting into.'

Lily placed her hands either side of his face and reached up on tiptoes to press a kiss to his lips. 'Nic, I trust you. You've done more for me these past few weeks than just about anyone else I can think of. You can say what you like, but if there's a crisis heading my way I know I want you there with me. Nothing you tell me about your past is going to change that.'

His face softened slightly, and she let herself hope for a moment that she'd got through to him.

'I want to do this,' she went on. 'I want us to take these feelings seriously. I'm not talking about sitting back and seeing what happens. I'm talking about working hard to make each other happy.'

He closed his eyes for a brief moment, and then leaned forward and kissed her quickly, sweetly.

'Can we walk?' he asked, keeping hold of her hand as he started moving again, towards the arch of sunlight at the end of the lane.

She said nothing, knowing that he was still working through his feelings.

'I don't know how I thought I could stop myself,' he said at last.

Lily bit her lip, wondering whether she was supposed to understand that enigmatic sentence.

'Falling for you, I mean.'

She risked a glance up at him and saw that it wasn't only tears that had made his eyes bright. There was a light there—something bright and shining. A smile that hadn't quite reached his lips yet but was lighting his face in a way that she recognised.

'You're sure that you don't want to get out now? Because I'd understand.'

'I'm going nowhere, Nic. But are *you* sure you're ready for his? Because I come as a package deal, remember?'

'I know that. I don't know how I thought I could fall for you without falling for Rosie as well, but I tried—and I failed. I want you for everything you are. And that includes the way you care for Rosie.'

'And you're okay with that?'

By his own admission he'd been fighting it, and fighting it hard. How could he be so sure now?

'I'm not going to lie and say that it doesn't hurt. Sometimes when I look at Rosie, growing all bonny and fat and healthy, it does make me think of my son and everything that he and I missed. But it's too late, Lily. She's a part of you, and I feel like she's becoming a part of me too.'

She was falling for him too—she knew that. The feelings that had been growing these past few weeks had only one possible end point. She smiled up at him and saw relief wash over his features as she reached up to kiss him, pressing her lips hard against his, trying to show with her body what she couldn't find the words to express.

They wandered the city hand in hand for another hour or two, with Rosie alternately snoozing or cooing from her baby carrier. The Trevi Fountain was magical, even packed with tourists, and the coffee in a little *piazza* café was hot and strong—but it was the light in Nic's eyes that made the afternoon perfect...the way he sneaked touches and kisses when they found themselves alone, the promise in his eyes and his body and the feelings for her that he had already declared.

When Rosie began to grumble, a little tired, they headed back to the hotel. Once she was tucked into her carrycot, all ready to be clipped into her pram when they went out for dinner, Lily headed out into the living room, a little nervous to be alone in a hotel room with Nic after all that had been said, all that had been resolved between them. She found Nic by the sofa, pouring glasses of something deliciously cold and sparkling.

'Something to start our evening off with a bit of a pop,' he said as she approached. 'Nonna's expecting us in about an hour, but if you need a bit more time…?'

Lily glanced at her watch. 'I think Rosie will sleep for another two hours at least, so as long as we don't have to disturb her that should be perfect. Just enough time to shower and change.'

Nic raised an eyebrow. 'You know you look perfect as you are.'

Lily had to laugh. He must have it bad, she thought, knowing full well that there was formula on her T-shirt and that she'd perspired more than was strictly lady-like during their walk.

'Don't give me that look,' Nic admonished. 'You could go out without doing a thing and be the envy of every woman in Rome.'

'Flattery will get you everywhere.'

She said the words without thinking, with a chuckle and a sip of her wine. But when she lowered her glass and met Nic's eyes it was to find them full of the passion they'd barely been suppressing all afternoon.

'An hour?' she asked, thinking of everything they could do in that time—all the possibilities open to them now they had admitted what they were feeling for one another.

'An hour's not nearly enough time for everything I've been thinking of,' Nic said, his face full of promise. 'And I think I might want a good meal first…'

Now, *that* sounded encouraging: the sort of evening one needed to carbo-load for.

Nic crossed the room until he was by her side and took the glass of Prosecco from her hands, placing it carefully on a side table before taking her in his arms. One hand sneaked up her spine and rested at the nape of her neck, the other settled in the small of her back, pulling her close against his hard body.

She let out a breathless sigh, wondering how they were meant to make it out of this hotel room without things getting out of hand. Reaching up, she cupped Nic's face in her palm, enjoying the rasp of his stubble against the smooth pads of her fingers, the hardness of his jaw and the softness of his cheeks. When her fingertips found his mouth, he kissed first one finger then the next.

With her thumb she explored the fullness of his bottom lip and the cleft of his chin. When she felt she knew every inch of his face she stretched up on tiptoes and traced the path of her fingers with her lips. Butterfly kisses that teased and promised more, but she wanted to savour every moment. They had all night to explore one another. And while there were parts of him she was desperate to know better, she was determined to make the most of every minute with him. Not to rush a single second of the experience.

For so many years she had waited, wondering when it would be her turn to have a family of her own. Now that she had found it she wanted to remember every moment, appreciate every sensation. Finally her lips found his, and she brushed a gentle kiss across his top lip, and then the bottom. Nic's fingers flexed behind her head, twisting strands of hair but not pressing her closer, not taking what she wasn't ready to give.

His body was strung like a bow, and with every caress she felt more tension in his muscles, more possession in his hold at the small of her back. When her thumb brushed the sensitive skin behind his ear his mouth opened in a groan, and she could resist temptation no longer.

She explored the warmth of his mouth, tested the limits of his restraint, measuring the desperation in his hold. The man was determined—she had to give him that. He'd said they should wait, and it seemed that wait they would. But she had only just started exploring, and at a guess they still had a good forty minutes before they had to leave.

When her tongue touched his, the fire she'd banked in his veins burst free. With the passion she'd seen in him earlier he possessed her mouth, his hands roaming now, rather than settling her against him. One dropped to the curve of her buttock, alternately caressing, exploring and pressing her against him. The other moved from nape to collarbone, and then lower. When his thumb brushed against her breast she moaned into his mouth, sure that at last she was going to get everything she had been fantasising about for the past month.

But he broke off their kiss, moved fractionally backwards until there was a good inch of space between them.

'You…are an absolute…siren.'

She gave him her most minxy smile as he struggled to speak, his voice ragged and breathless.

'And I am going to make you pay for that later. But for now a shower—a cold one, I suggest—and then let's go to dinner.'

'Spoilsport.'

But she couldn't be disappointed really—not when she'd seen the effect she'd had on him, and now knew better than ever what she had in store when they got home. Waiting had done nothing to temper their passion before now, and another couple of hours could only make them more ardent.

She hadn't known what to expect of Nonna's *pensione*, and at times when they'd passed by the brightly lit windows of the Trastevere area she'd feared that they would find themselves in either a fine dining restaurant, where she would feel awkward and out of place, or one of the *trattorie* designed to trap tourists—all plastic vegetables and fake bonhomie. But when she walked through the door of Nonna's her fears instantly vanished.

This was neither pretentious nor tacky. It was— almost instantly—*home*. The moment they walked through the door she found herself enfolded in a generous matronly bosom and kissed on both her cheeks. Nic had pushed the pram across the challenging Roman cobbles and was now wrestling it up the front steps, leaving Lily undefended against this friendly onslaught.

'*Bella*, you are the friend of Nico. You are so very welcome tonight,' she said, kissing her again on both cheeks.

'Signora Lucia, it's a pleasure to meet you.'

'*Tsch*, you must call me Nonna—like my Nico.'

At that, Nic finally made it up the steps with the carrycot, and Nonna's attention was lost completely as she peered into the carrycot and spoke in a loud whisper.

'And your *bambina*. She is a beauty. Nico told me this and now I see. *Bella*—like her *mamma*.'

Lily blushed, both from the compliment and the mix-up. But she was distracted from correcting her by the sensation of Nic's arm settling across her shoulders. The gesture was comforting, possessive, natural, and she turned into the warmth of his body.

Nonna bent over the pram again and Lily held her breath, hoping that the baby wouldn't wake up and fret through their dinner, but Nonna only stroked her cheek and muttered a string of Italian babytalk.

'Come—I have lovely table for this lovely family,' she said, and she stood and led them to a table set for two, tucked in a private corner. A candle flickered on the crisply ironed cloth and Nonna pulled up a bench for them to set the carrycot on.

'When she wakes up you call me and I come see her, okay?'

Lily was filled with such a sense of warmth and welcome that she felt tears welling behind her eyes.

'You didn't correct her,' Nic said, his voice carefully casual, and Lily knew he was referring to Nonna's use of the word *'mamma'*.

'I didn't really know what to say…how to explain… Anyway, you distracted me.'

'Me? What did I do?'

'That casual arm around the shoulder. I couldn't think for a minute.'

'An *arm*? After what you tried earlier, you couldn't think because of an arm?'

She laughed. 'Well, maybe the arm brought back a memory or two,' she clarified. 'What must she think of me? A mum with a new baby, out for dinner with a man who's not the father. Wait—she knows you're not Rosie's dad, right?'

Nic took a sip of the Prosecco that Nonna had poured when she'd shown them to their table. 'She knows. And I think it's as clear to you as it is to me that she already adores you both. She doesn't care about the details of how Rosie came into our life any more than I do. She can see that you love her like a mother.'

'But I'm not, am I? Rosie and I have spent all this time getting to know each other, trying to see how our lives can fit together, and it could all have been for nothing. We could get back to London and find that everything's changed. I could lose Rosie—and then what?'

'First,' Nic said, pressing her hand into his, 'I'm sure that whatever happens with Helen you're never going to lose Rosie completely. I think that your sister loves you, and loves Rosie, and she knows that you're both better off with each other in your lives. If Helen was to turn up tomorrow and take Rosie away—we'd try and cope…together.'

She took a deep breath, forcing her body to relax. She wasn't sure where the sudden surge of fear and apprehension had come from. Perhaps it was inevitable, she thought. With things going so well in one part of her life now that she and Nic seemed to be finally finding their way towards happiness, some other aspect of it had to fall apart. Surely this was too good to be true—

a kind, handsome man, a romantic getaway in Rome, a beautiful niece whom she thought of as a daughter...

'Are you okay?' Nic asked, concern creasing his forehead.

Lily nodded, determined to throw off this sense that it was all going too well. It would be unforgivable to ruin this evening just because of some strange sense of foreboding. There was no such thing as karma. The universe wasn't going to punish her for being happy with Nic by taking Rosie away.

'Better than okay,' she said, and after glancing around to check that no one was looking she sneaked a quick kiss. 'Sorry—just a wobble. I guess I'm still not quite sure what I am to Rosie—mum or aunty. It's going to take a little time to get used to what other people might think.'

'It doesn't matter what anyone else thinks. What matters is that you and Rosie are happy.'

'Well, we are. Blissfully,' she replied honestly. 'This has been just a perfect day, Nic. I don't know how to thank you.'

'Oh, well, I can think of an idea or two,' he replied with a cheeky grin. 'But there's no need to thank me. The pleasure of your company for today is thanks enough.'

She smiled back, and then turned her head as Rosie stirred in her cot.

'Will she wake soon?' Nic asked.

'Maybe just for a feed, but she normally goes back to sleep after a bit of a cuddle.'

'She's changing so quickly,' Nic said, watching her as she wriggled awake.

Lily reached out and touched his arm, knowing that

he was thinking of Max. But he wasn't frowning when she looked up at him. Instead he had the same soppy, dopey expression that she normally wore when she was talking about Rosie.

'It's amazing to watch her, you know. I feel very lucky to be a part of it.'

'We feel pretty lucky too,' Lily told him. 'I know how hard you've found it, but having you here for me these past few weeks…I'm not sure what I would have done without you.'

'You'd have done fine,' he told her. 'But you're right. Some things are better when you can share them with someone.'

'I'm glad you said that,' Lily said, trying to lighten the mood. 'Because I have to nip to the bathroom. Are you okay with her for a minute?'

Before today she'd have watched him carefully, trying to judge his reaction to the thought of being left alone with Rosie. But now she trusted him to tell her what he was feeling. To tell her if she was asking too much.

'Of course.'

He pulled her down for a brief kiss as she passed him, and she was filled with a sense of warmth and well-being.

When she returned from the bathroom it was to find Nonna seated at their table with the baby on her lap drinking from her bottle and lapping up the attention. She moved to stand beside Nic, but when she arrived Nonna stood, offering her her seat back.

'I cannot resist such a beautiful baby,' she told Lily. 'Nico tells me she's hungry and I find myself sitting

like this. I think I'll never put her down. She is so wonderful I keep her for ever.'

'I hope she wasn't causing trouble?' Lily replied.

'Not at all,' Nic reassured her. 'Nonna just couldn't
resist. I hope that's okay?'

She told him that of course it was, and when a shout
emerged from the kitchen both Nic and Lily held out
their hands to take the baby.

Lily could almost feel the weight of her in her hands,
but Nonna passed her to Nic instead, and Lily was left
watching as Rosie settled happily into his arms.

'Ah… Daddy's girl, I think you say. I must go back
to the kitchen now, but if she cries I will come straight
away and take her. You two need a quiet dinner. Lots
of talking,' Nonna commented sagely, before bustling
in the direction of the kitchen.

Lily watched as Nonna walked away, her mouth
slightly open in surprise.

'What can I say?' Nick commented with a laugh.
'She's quite a force. I'm always too terrified to argue
with her. I think she's crazy about you, though.'

'Crazy, perhaps,' Lily agreed. 'You didn't even
flinch,' she said, 'when she said Daddy.'

He took a deep breath, and Lily knew that he was
working up to something.

'You know that I've never thought about having any
more children, but when Nonna said that my initial reaction wasn't horror or fear. Instead I thought about
how much I liked being a dad. How I might like that
again one day.'

Lily couldn't speak. She'd paused with her glass
halfway to her lips and now found that she couldn't
move. Was he talking about starting a family? With

her? For a fleeting second she could see it—the three of them, the four of them…God, maybe even more—but then a gentle panic started to nag. Things were moving too quickly, surely, to be talking about this now.

'I didn't mean right away,' he said, interpreting her expression. 'I just meant that one day I think I might want it again. And I've never thought that before.'

Lily finally took the sip of her wine, buying herself a few more moments to calm herself.

'I'm glad if me and Rosie have helped.'

The words sounded trite, even to her, and she wondered how she had wandered into this politeness— wondered at the distance that seemed to have sprung from nowhere.

She *wanted* Nic to want a family. Deep down, she wanted Nic to be part of *her* family. Surely that was what it was all about? Getting to know someone, exploring a relationship. She'd always envisaged marriage, a husband. Equal partners. But now she wondered if she'd really thought about what that would mean. She'd never considered that her family growing meant that she was a smaller constituent part. Since Rosie had landed on her doorstep she'd been everything to her, and it was going to take some getting used to if she wanted Rosie to share her affections with someone else.

She wanted to show that she could do it herself. Wanted to build a family and keep it close. What did it say about her if she couldn't do it? If one day she wasn't the person Rosie turned to?

Their starters arrived and she ate, watching Nic and Rosie, despising the curl of jealousy she couldn't deny, despite the fact that she knew it was ridiculous. She pasted on a smile, not wanting Nic to guess that her thoughts were still dwelling on Rosie's willingness to go to him. It was just one bottle, she reminded herself. Not a competition, or anything.

Rosie finished her bottle with an enthusiastic gurgle, and the familiar sound broke Lily's tense mood.

'Do you want to take her?' Nic asked, looking a little hesitant.

Well, maybe she hadn't hidden her worries as well as she had hoped.

'You cuddle a little longer if you want to,' Lily said—and meant it. How could she begrudge these two some time together? Rosie deserved this full-on attention—deserved the full force of Nic's smile and the warmth and comfort of his arms. There was a connection between the two of them, Lily acknowledged, and she was glad of it.

'So, did you tell your sister about this little excursion?' Lily asked, finding it a little strange that Kate hadn't called for a run-down of the latest developments.

'Well, it all happened so fast...' Nic said with an expression of insincere innocence. 'I only just managed to tell her that I had to go away. There simply wasn't time to tell her that you two were coming as well.'

'By which I take it to mean you were too scared to confess?'

He laughed. 'The woman's capacity for inappropriate questions knows no bounds,' he said, holding up his hands in defeat. 'It takes a stronger man than I am to volunteer for that sort of grilling.'

'Oh, gee, thanks—so you leave me to handle the fall-out when we get back?'

'Is there a chance that she might just conveniently never find out?' Nic asked, looking hopeful.

'Not any chance, I'm afraid. You're right—she sniffs these things out, and if she ever discovered that I'd kept it from her there'd be hell to pay. *So* not worth it. She has to forgive *you*—you're her brother. If I held back on her I'm not sure that she'd ever take me back.'

Nic laughed. 'I'm not so sure about that. Some of the lectures I've endured—I think she's rather more concerned with you than with me.'

Lily could imagine. Kate was protective of her friends at the best of times, but since Rosie had come on the scene, and Lily's life had become at least twenty-seven thousand times more complicated, she'd stepped things up a level. Lily had tried telling her that she didn't need to worry so much, but Kate seemed determined to be the gatekeeper to Lily's life.

Conversation flowed like wine through the rest of their dinner, and by the time Nonna was cooing over Rosie as she brought over their coffees the earlier tension had disappeared completely. Well, not *disappeared*, exactly. It had morphed into a different sort of tension.

The sort that drew her close to Nic's side as he manoeuvred the pram back to the hotel. The sort that had her up on her tiptoes and stealing a quick, hard kiss in the hotel lift. And the sort that made her draw away from him, a little shy, once they'd reached the privacy of their suite.

But her kiss in the lift had clearly fired something in Nic, and the moment they were through the door his arms were around her, lifting her and moulding her, until his lean body was perfectly fitted to her soft curves and his lips had found hers in a kiss that stole her breath.

All thoughts of shyness fled under the onslaught of sensation: hips and lips on hers, his hands in her hair, the cold wood of the door behind her back contrasting with the heat of his body. She tore her lips away and tilted her head, inviting him to kiss the soft skin of her neck. He responded greedily, nuzzling at her collarbone, sipping kisses from behind her ear, biting gently on her shoulder.

She let out a groan as she let her body loosen, her weight held entirely by door and man, and instead focussed her energy on Nic, on kissing and exploring and reaching bare skin.

Until a snuffle from the pram behind him drew her up short.

Her body froze instantly and Nic backed away, a question in his eyes.

'Sorry...' she gasped, fighting for reason as much as she was for breath. 'I nearly forgot...' How could she have forgotten that Rosie was right there? That she was responsible for a little human life before giving in to her own needs and desires?

But Nic didn't look concerned, or even shocked that she had put her own passions above her responsibility to Rosie.

'Don't worry about it,' he said, kissing her again on the lips, but gently this time. 'She was fast asleep and perfectly safe. You didn't do anything wrong.'

She let out a long breath, thankful to have this understanding, intelligent man in her life. Someone who saw her worst fears even more clearly than she saw them herself.

'Why don't you get her settled? Take your time,' he added, with an expression full of dark, seductive promise. 'I'm not going anywhere.'

Take your time. Why had he said that? It seemed as if she'd been in her bedroom for an age, and he paced the living room, waiting for her to return. He could hear Rosie, grizzling slightly—disturbed, he guessed, by the move from warm pram to cold cot. *Settle quickly*, he pleaded with her silently, desperate to pick up where he and Lily had left off.

He poured wine, for the sake of something to do, though he knew that they wouldn't touch it. He'd sipped one glass all night and Lily had barely started hers.

Finally the door to Lily's room opened, and he turned on the spot to see her closing it softly, peeking through at the last minute to make sure that Rosie was okay. With barely a whisper the latch closed, and they were alone at last.

He forced himself to stay where he was—not to rush over and hold her against the wall as he had earlier. He'd moved quickly—too quickly—when they'd first arrived back, and she'd ended up looking uncertain and concerned. He couldn't risk that again. Instead he'd wait for her to come to him, as she had before they'd gone out for dinner, teasing him with her kisses and caresses.

She crossed the room to stand in front of him, but kept her body from him still. He stood firm, determined that she must reach for him and not the other way around. She'd dropped her eyes. He loved to see bashfulness warring with passion in her posture and in her features. Was she having second thoughts? God knew *he'd* had enough over the past few weeks. But none tonight. He wouldn't ever again, he suspected, after his revelation this afternoon of what she'd come to mean to him.

Caving at last, unable to keep himself from touching her, he brushed his lips gently across her cheek. 'Everything okay?' he asked gently.

'Fine,' Lily said, finally looking up.

Her smile was brave, but not entirely genuine. There was still something troubling her, he knew.

'What is it?' he asked, pulling on her hand until she dropped down next to him on the sofa.

'Nothing's wrong,' she said, but then paused. 'It's just hard…trying to do what's right for Rosie and what I want for me.'

'Those two things aren't mutually exclusive, you know,' he told her gently.

'I know. But when we came in just now I just wasn't thinking. I mean *at all*. Anything could have happened and I'd have been completely oblivious.'

The smug smile was halfway to his lips before he got it under control.

'That's not true, Lily,' he reminded her. 'As soon as she made a peep you were right there. You can do a good job of taking care of her *and* have a life of your own as well. Trust me,' he said, wrapping an arm around her shoulder. 'You're doing an amazing job. But if you want to turn in now, cuddle up just the two of you in your room, then I would understand.'

She thought about it for a long minute.

'It's not what I want,' she told him, her voice carrying a slight waver. 'I know what I want—you.'

He breathed a long sigh of relief. He'd meant what

he'd said—he would have kissed her gently goodnight and watched her shut her bedroom door behind her—but, God, was he glad that he didn't have to.

He'd wrapped his arm around her shoulder to comfort her, but as his fingers brushed across the soft skin of her upper arm the caress turned from soothing to sensual, and his fingertips crackled with the electricity that surged between them.

Lily turned to him, but he knew the next move had to come from her. If she'd had doubts—if she *still* had doubts—he'd understand, and he wouldn't rush her.

Slowly, quietly, she moved closer to him, until her lips were just an inch from his, the lower one caught between her teeth. He could bite it for her, he thought, imagining the warmth and moistness of her mouth. She looked from his eyes to his lips and reached out her hand. Her thumb caught his lower lip, as it had earlier, caressing gently. He opened his mouth to her, inviting her in, and finally, excruciatingly, she leaned forward and pressed her lips to his. But it wasn't surrender on her part—it was triumph as she kissed and tasted and explored.

He ran his hands down to her hips, pulling her closer to him, and swallowed the satisfied groan that emerged from her mouth. Now, with no distractions, no limits on their time, no reason not to do everything he had ever imagined…it was intoxicating. He pulled her closer still, until she was nestled onto his lap, her arms around his neck. When he could hold back no longer he stood, lifting her as if she weighed no more than a feather, and started towards his bedroom.

She pulled back for a moment and gazed into his

eyes. 'Yes?' he asked, hoping with every part of his being that he had judged this right.

'Oh, God, yes,' Lily replied, her voice barely more than a husky murmur. *'Yes.'*

CHAPTER THIRTEEN

LILY CRACKED AN eyelid and glanced at the clock on the bedside table—it was nearly six. Rosie would be up again soon, and Lily didn't want her to wake up alone in a strange place. She eased herself out from under Nic's arm, careful not to wake him, and threw on what she could find of her clothes. She sneaked out of the room, closing the door softly behind her.

Rosie was awake when she went into their room, happily gurgling in her cot. 'Morning, sunshine,' she whispered as she got closer. 'Did you remember we're on holiday?'

She picked up the phone and arranged for hot water to be brought up, then started digging in Rosie's bag for formula and a bottle.

Once she'd answered the discreet knock at the door and made up Rosie's breakfast she wasn't sure what to do next. In the night she'd fed Rosie in bed, and then crept back to Nic and initiated round two, and three… What if Nic woke this time and found her gone? It didn't seem like the right way to start their day. But bringing Rosie into their bed—it screamed *family*, and she wasn't sure if they were ready for that.

I'll go back to him, she decided eventually. It might

not be the right thing to do—there was no way to know until she did it—but getting back into her cold bed alone didn't seem like the right thing, either.

She tiptoed back into Nic's room, trying not to wake him as she eased herself under the blankets without dropping either baby or bottle.

She settled into the pillows and looked around her. This was it, she thought. Beautiful baby…beautiful man. This was how she had always imagined Sunday mornings would be. Admittedly, their path to here had been a little unconventional, and, yes, it was a Thursday, but now she was here it seemed pretty perfect to her.

It was almost impossible not to reach out and touch Nic. She wondered whether it was possible to wake him just by staring at him. Apparently not. But Rosie didn't have the same scruples as Lily and was more than happy to wake Nic up, practising a raspberry noise with a mouthful of milk. Lily tried to mop up without waking him, but the stirring hand beneath the sheet gave him away and she knew that Rosie had managed what she hadn't dared.

She watched his face as he swam up from sleep. A lazy smile lifted his lips as he realised she was there: he'd forgotten, perhaps. Though how he couldn't remember last night, when it was seared on her memory, she had no idea. His face fell when he spotted Rosie and he pulled himself up on the pillows, blinking rapidly and wiping sleep from his eyes with the heels of his hands.

'Morning.'

His voice was gruff, and not entirely friendly. She instinctively pulled the blankets a little tighter around them, feeling suddenly vulnerable under his scornful gaze. Was it her presence or Rosie's that was the problem? She knew the answer to that—he'd been more than happy to see *her*, it had only been when he'd spotted the baby that his face had turned to stone. And when his face had dropped, so had Lily's.

'Sorry, we didn't mean to wake you.'

She *was* sorry for waking him, but she didn't see that she really had anything else to apologise for. Nic was the one who had told her he was ready for this. That he'd struggled in the past but wanted her and Rosie to be a part of his life. He couldn't have expected her to sneak back to her own bed this morning as if nothing had happened, could he? Or to leave Rosie where she was and pretend that this wasn't the reality of her life?

Nic tried pasting a smile back on to his face but it was too late: the damage was done. The cracks were showing anyway, and Lily knew that however much he might say otherwise he wasn't as ready for this as he'd said he was. He would have been happier not to find them both there this morning, and that cracked Lily's heart more than just a little.

'No, it's fine—just a surprise, that's all.'

A surprise? It shouldn't have been. If he really understood her life—and how could he decide if he wanted to be a part of it if he didn't understand it?—then surely he should have expected this.

She hadn't known when she'd woken in the dawn light what to expect of this morning—whether they would be awkward, or whether the natural-as-breathing intimacy of last night would carry through to today.

The last thing she'd expected was this: the sight of Nic climbing from the bed and pulling running shorts from a drawer.

'I think I might make the most of the early-morning temperature,' he said, not meeting her eye. 'Fit in a quick jog before it hits thirty degrees. You don't mind, do you?'

Did it matter what she thought? It was pretty obvious that he was going, either way.

As the door to the bathroom shut she looked down at Rosie and breathed out a long sigh. Last night everything had seemed so perfect, so right. She had known even then that it was too good to be true.

Nic counted his breaths in and out as his feet struck the unfamiliar cobbles, trying to pace himself around the irregular maze of streets and alleyways. That was maybe the most cowardly thing he'd ever done, and no number of heel-strikes was going to make him any less ashamed of it. The look on Lily's face had been heartbreaking. A mixture of confusion and sorrow.

He pushed himself harder and checked his watch: he'd been gone forty-five minutes. The guilt was more than a twinge—it was closer to a knife in his gut. He really should go back. But what to say to her?

He'd seen her face. How could he make her see that he'd meant everything he'd said to her yesterday? When he'd told her he was falling for her, that he wanted both her *and* Rosie in his life, he'd meant it—and he'd thought he'd known what he was taking on.

But nothing had quite prepared him for the sight

of them both when he was barely awake, barely conscious. There had been a split second when he'd seen a different baby, when he'd been in a different bed. And the thought of what had happened, of the different reality that he was waking up to, had crushed his heart for a moment.

This was harder than he'd expected, but that didn't mean he was giving up. Anything worth having was worth fighting for. Hard. But how could Lily know that he felt that way? He'd already told her that he didn't know if she could rely on him, and now he'd gone and proved it—he'd bailed at the first opportunity. As far as she was concerned he'd got what he'd been looking for and then left her alone in his bed while he pulled on clothes and headed out through the door.

He turned back to the hotel, wondering what he'd find when he got there. Her bags packed, perhaps. Or the suite empty, her clothes gone from the wardrobe and her lotions missing from the bathroom.

He let himself into the suite and was relieved to hear her singing in her bedroom, Rosie gurgling along. There was clearly something about the combination of nursery rhymes and power ballads that was irresistible to that girl.

Obviously encouraged, Lily turned up the volume and sang even louder. The door was open and he crossed the living room, resting his shoulder against the frame as he watched her dancing around, pulling faces to try and make Rosie smile. Despite his serious mood, he found himself smiling too.

But he knew that he was intruding on something personal, so he cleared his throat, drawing her attention. Colour rose on her cheeks as she turned towards him, and she stopped singing instantly.

'You're back.'

'Yes. And I'm sorry for leaving like that.'

She dropped her gaze, but not before he could see the hurt in her eyes. He had a lot of explaining to do—and a lot of making up. For weeks they'd been moving so slowly, feeling their way towards trusting each other, and then with one rash move—running instead of staying and explaining—he'd destroyed something of the bond they'd built. Had he learnt nothing from the way things had ended with Clare?

'Are you hungry?' he asked. 'I thought we could call down for some breakfast and eat up here. I know that I've upset you, and I think it would be good to talk.'

She didn't answer for a moment; instead she picked up Rosie from the bed and held her against her chest. Her arms were firm around her, and Nic knew that the cuddle was more for Lily's comfort than for Rosie's.

'Sure,' she said eventually. 'I'll order something while you take a shower.'

He washed quickly. Part of him wanted to delay this conversation—delay the moment when he had to look at Lily and know how much his selfishness had hurt her. But it wasn't fair on her to make her wait longer than she already had for his apology and his explanation. So he grabbed a towel and dragged it over his limbs.

The softness of the cotton reminded him of her tender caresses last night—the way that every sensation had been heightened until even the brush of the sheet against his back had driven him to heights he hadn't recognised.

He glanced at the clock as he walked towards his wardrobe. He had meetings today—it was why he was here, after all—but the thought that he'd have to leave in an hour, whether things were settled or not, twisted that knife in his gut.

When he arrived back in the living room a waiter was laying a breakfast of pastries, cold meat and absurdly good-smelling coffee on the table by the window. Lily was standing, looking out over the city, Rosie still in her arms. She had grabbed a handful of Lily's hair, and Lily was gently teasing her as she eased it out of her grasp.

She turned—must have heard his footsteps—and the smile dropped from her face at the sight of him. She looked guarded, wary, as if about to do battle.

'This looks nice,' he told her, and could have kicked himself for hiding behind pleasantries.

She just nodded—didn't even answer as she settled Rosie into the bouncy chair by the table and then sat herself.

'Lily, I'm sorry,' he said as soon as the waiter had left the room. 'I shouldn't have just taken off like that. You have every right to be angry with me.'

She nodded—which didn't do much to help the guilt in his belly.

'I should have stayed to talk to you, to explain what I was feeling.'

She met his gaze head-on and nodded. It was everything he'd feared. Everything he'd warned her of. He'd let her down.

'Right. You should.'

Good. She wasn't going to make this easy on him. He didn't deserve *easy*. He deserved to see how his actions had affected her. This was what he wanted. To be Lily's lover and partner. Maybe—if he could fix this unholy mess he'd made—more. He couldn't expect all that without giving everything of himself in return.

'Why did you go?' she asked.

He tried to find the right words to express what he had felt, to tell her that he'd been hurt but it hadn't been her fault.

'It was seeing you and Rosie like that, when I was barely awake. It just brought back...memories.'

Her face softened and relief swept through him like a wave. She understood. He'd known deep down that she would. She wouldn't be the woman he thought she was if she wasn't able to sympathise with another person's pain. But that didn't make what he'd done right. He should have spoken to her, explained what he was feeling, rather than running from the pain and from her. That was what he'd done at the start, when he'd first met her. If he couldn't show her that things had changed, if he *hadn't* changed, then what chance would he have of showing her that they could be happy together.

She nodded. 'I understand,' she said.

And maybe she did. But that didn't mean she'd forgiven him. She picked at her pastry, and he knew that hurt was still simmering under the surface.

'But you could have asked for my help, my support.' She gave him a long look before she spoke again. 'What are we to each other if we can't do that?'

What are we to each other? Genuinely, he didn't know. Had he been naïve, thinking that they could make a relationship out of good intentions? Maybe there was too much history, too much pain. After all, he'd been tested once and hadn't come out of it well. But the only way to know was by trying, and so far things weren't looking great.

'This is why me and Clare…' he started. 'I couldn't talk. She needed me to. I tried. I couldn't.'

She let out an exasperated sigh. 'I don't want to hear again that you let Clare down because you wouldn't talk to her about how you were feeling. It wasn't fair of her to expect you to grieve the way she wanted you to. I wasn't planning on making you do anything you weren't comfortable with this morning. But instead of finding that out you decided to bail. You don't have to talk to me about your feelings for your son, but if we can't find a way to communicate with each other then we're lost before we've even really started.'

Her words made him stop his pacing. He'd never considered that maybe there was another side to what had happened in his last relationship. That perhaps he wasn't entirely to blame. If only the same could be said about this morning.

From the corner of his eye he caught sight of the clock on the wall and cursed under his breath.

Lily followed his eyeline. 'Your meeting,' she said, remembering.

'I don't have to leave just yet.'

'But you'll be late if you leave it much longer. It wouldn't exactly give the right impression. If you don't get this contract signed then what was the point of us coming here? You should go.'

What was the point of them coming here? Could she not see that the whole thing had been his—clearly misjudged—way of contriving to find some time for them to get to know each other? The whole point of this trip was *them*, not the business.

But she was already heading back to her room, and he didn't have to ask to know that he wasn't invited to follow her.

CHAPTER FOURTEEN

THE HOTEL DOOR closed behind Nic and she breathed out a long sigh—disappointment? Relief? She wasn't sure. Her heart had started hurting the moment he'd left the suite earlier that morning and hadn't stopped since. His brief return and apology hadn't helped. It wasn't that she didn't forgive him—he'd clearly been in pain, and she could understand and sympathise with that. But instead of asking her to face that pain *with* him, trying to find a way to get past those feelings *together*, he had turned from her. Literally run from her.

Twenty-four hours in Rome. Well, their time was nearly up. By the time Nic got back from his meeting she'd need her bags packed and ready to go, and they'd have to go straight to the airport. There was no time to fix this before they had to leave, and her shoulders slumped with sadness that a day as sweet and as perfect as yesterday could be tarnished so soon.

Rosie had gone back to sleep, so she moved around the room quietly, tucking her belongings into bags and cases, checking under the bed and in the bathroom drawers.

Rosie gave a whimpering little cry in her sleep, a sound Lily didn't recognise, and she stopped her packing and crossed to the cot. Whatever had upset her hadn't been enough to wake her properly, and she'd settled herself back to sleep, but Lily watched her a little longer, feeling a swell of trepidation. It was just the remnants of her disagreement with Nic, she reasoned. Making her see trouble where there was none.

Rosie gave another sniffle, and this time Lily reached into her cot to check that she wasn't too hot. The air-con was on, and the thermostat was showing a perfect eighteen degrees, but her skin was just a little clammy and warm. Lily pulled the blanket back, so that Rosie was left under just a sheet, and then dug the thermometer out of the first aid kit she had brought with her.

Rosie's temperature was on the high side of normal. Maybe she'd picked up a cold, Lily thought, trying not to let her mind race ahead. She had some infant paracetamol in her case, and she woke the baby to feed her some. She barely opened her eyes, but swallowed down the medicine, and Lily told herself just to keep an eye on things and not to panic as she rocked her gently.

Nic arrived back from his meeting and she could see from his face that it had gone according to plan. That was something, at least. And the paracetamol had seemed to do the trick with Rosie. Her temperature had returned to normal, and she seemed to be sleeping easier.

A maid had turned up to pack Nic's things, so by the time he was back they were all but ready to go. They stood in the living room, their cases at their feet as they waited for a porter, and Lily wondered if they would ever rediscover the intimacy they had felt yesterday. Perhaps she had overreacted when Nic had left this morning, but it wasn't just her sadness and disappointment that was between them. It was more than that. At the first instance of something hard in their relationship Nic had decided to leave rather than work at it.

Yesterday they had been full of optimism about the future—aware of the challenges they might face, but ready to tackle them together. This morning had shattered that illusion.

Nic wanted to face his demons alone, and so must she.

She'd worked so hard to be a good mother to Rosie that she knew she could do it alone, that she didn't need Nic by her side to be a good parent, to hold her and Rosie together in their little family. She just needed to remember that. Remember that the most important thing in all of this was to be a good mother. Everything else came second. If that meant protecting Rosie from someone who wasn't ready to be in her life then she would have to do that, however much it hurt.

The flight had been short and uneventful, their way smoothed by Nic's charm and first-class tickets. Again his preparations had been thorough, and the onboard staff had responded to everything Rosie had needed, though she had slept for most of the flight. Lily had kept thermometer and paracetamol in her handbag, and kept a careful eye on her, looking out for any signs that this might be more than a cold.

Nic had asked her more than once if she was okay, if Rosie was okay, if there was anything that he could do. She'd smiled and said no thanks, needing to focus on Rosie. With her baby still grizzly and unhappy there was no time or space in her head to tackle this frosty wasteland that was expanding between them.

Now, in the luggage hall, Rosie started crying feebly, and it didn't seem to matter what Lily did—she paced, she rocked, she bounced—she wouldn't stop. She took her temperature again, and as soon as she saw the number on the little digital display—nearly two degrees higher than when she'd last taken it—she was reaching for the phone.

She dialled the NHS urgent helpline and bit her lip with nerves as she waited for her call to be taken. Nic guided her through the airport and out to their car as she answered the operator's questions, telling her what Rosie's temperature was and how sleepy she'd been.

The car pulled away from the airport and she barely even noticed. She had no time or energy to mark the end of their trip. Her ear was glued to her phone, and her eyes flitted between Rosie and the thermometer. She cast Nic the occasional glance and noted that he looked grey, drawn. No wonder, she thought, given everything he had been through.

But she had to focus on Rosie. She had to funnel out Nic's pain and concentrate on her girl.

Finally, after running through a seemingly endless list of questions, the operator spoke in a calming, measured voice that made Lily instantly terrified.

'Now, I know that you're in the car, so what I'm going to suggest is that you go to the nearest hospital with an Accident and Emergency department. If you can give me your location I'll be able to let you know where that is. Or if you want to pull over I'll arrange for an ambulance to come to you.'

Lily had never believed that a person could feel their

own heart stop, but in that moment she could have sworn her every bodily function ceased. She didn't breathe, blood stopped flowing in her veins, she stilled completely.

'Lily, love, are you still there?'

She nodded, before finding her voice and asking the driver for their exact location, then relaying it to the operator on the phone.

Lily thanked her for her help and hung up. She turned back to Rosie, who was sleepy, but still grizzling in her car seat.

'Lily?'

She could barely bring herself to look at Nic, because she needed to focus with everything that she had on Rosie. She had to give her her full attention. She couldn't bear to lose another member of her family—and this time she knew if it happened she would be the only one to blame. She was solely responsible for taking care of Rosie, and she had to make sure that she got better. If she didn't…it wouldn't just be Rosie she was losing. How could she ever face her sister again if she let anything happen to her?

'Lily, what's going on?' Nic asked.

She turned towards him but couldn't meet his eye. Instead she kept her gaze around his jaw, noted the tension there, and the pallor of his skin, but couldn't let herself worry about that now. Couldn't let herself think of anything but Rosie.

'We have to go straight to a hospital,' she told him. 'They didn't say what they thought might be wrong, but they want her checked out asap.'

'Three minutes,' their driver called from the front seat. 'Hospital's just up ahead and there's no traffic.'

Lily couldn't allow herself an ounce of relief. She had to stay alert, stay ready, make sure that she was focussed only on her little girl.

Nic reached for her hand and squeezed it gently. 'Lily, I'm sure they're just being cautious. Rosie's going to be fine.'

She opened her mouth to answer, but her voice wasn't there. Instead tears were welling in her eyes and threatening a flood. She couldn't do this. Not with him here. Not with his fear of the worst-case scenario written so plainly on his features. Her only responsibility was taking care of her family, and Nic had told her and then proved this morning that when things were tough he wasn't going to be there for her.

Lily unbuckled her seatbelt and put her hands on the straps of Rosie's car seat, ready to have her out of there as soon as the car pulled up outside A&E.

The click of Nic's seatbelt being unbuckled drew her attention, and she glanced over at him. 'You don't need to come in.'

'It's okay,' he said, though the dread and fear in his face told a different story.

'No.' Lily took a deep breath, knowing that she had to do this—for her niece, for her family, for herself. 'I can do this on my own,' she said firmly.

Nic stared at her, clearly shocked. Was there relief there too? she wondered. There must be. He'd never wanted to get involved with a family…never wanted to expose himself to the hurt and pain that might be waiting for them around the corner. She couldn't make him do this for her, and she couldn't walk into that hospital with someone who might bail on her at any moment. It was better to do this now, end things here, and know exactly where she stood, exactly who she could rely on as she walked into the hospital.

'I'll come in with you, Lily. You shouldn't have to do this by yourself.'

But she didn't want him there out of duty or obligation—didn't want him there against his better judgement. She wanted him there because he was part of her, part of Rosie. Because they were a family. He was offering half-measures, and that just wasn't good enough. Not for her, and not for Rosie.

'No!' Lily shouted this time, the tears finally spilling onto her cheeks. 'We're better off on our own,' she blurted. 'And not just today. We made a mistake, Nic. This was never going to work. We're better off accepting that now, before it goes any further. You know I'm right. You know that you don't want to be inside that hospital with us. I'm sorry, but it's for the best. It's over, Nic.'

As they came to an abrupt halt Lily grabbed for Rosie, lifting her out of the car seat. The driver opened the door behind her and she ran from the car, focussing on Rosie's face, refusing to look back.

CHAPTER FIFTEEN

LILY UNLOCKED THE door to Kate's flat one-handed while Rosie slept peacefully at last in the crook of her arm. She'd never used her friend's key without asking before, but with her own place still a building site and her relationship with Nic in tatters she had nowhere else to go.

It had been a long couple of days. She wished she could curl up like Rosie, block out the world and sleep through the day. The last seventy-two hours had consisted of nail-biting terror and endless waiting while doctors drew blood, ran tests, muttered together in corners.

Until this morning, when a smiling junior doctor had come to give her the news—all clear. They had been worried about meningitis, they'd told her when she'd arrived at the hospital, and had run a slew of tests. But every one had come back negative. It seemed that Rosie had been battling a nasty case of flu, and after three days of topping her up with fluids and paracetamol they were happy for her to be discharged.

After settling Rosie in her carrycot she plugged in her phone, dreading what might be waiting for her there. Nic had called a couple of times, and then passed the baton on to Kate. But Lily had found that she didn't know what to say. She'd breathed a sigh of relief when the phone's battery had died and she'd not had to think about it any more.

But now that she was back, and Rosie was on the mend, she knew that she had some thinking to do. And—she suspected—some apologising. Kate, for one, would be furious that she'd been incommunicado for more than twenty-four hours. And Nic...?

She had no idea what she could expect from him— if anything. Looking back at that car journey, she was ashamed of the way she had behaved, and saw in her behaviour a reflection of his, of everything she had criticised him for that very morning. She'd not talked about what was scaring her; she'd not tried to explain. Instead she'd decided that she had to do things on her own, in her own way, and left him out in the cold while she got on with it.

But the thing really twisting the knife in her stomach was the fact that she knew he had been hurting already. Seeing Rosie sick, the trip to the hospital, the not knowing what was happening... It must have brought back so many memories. And instead of trying to help, or even to understand, she'd pushed him away.

Just as she was putting on the kettle, hoping that coffee would make this awful day better, a key turned in the front door. Kate, home from work. Or Nic? she thought suddenly, with a stab of guilt in her belly. Did he have a key to his sister's place?

She thought for a moment about trying to sneak out the back way. But her best friend and her brother had stood by her these last few weeks—the most challenging of her life—and it would be cruel of her to push them away now. The thought of facing Nic's hurt and Kate's disapproval was terrifying, but it couldn't be put off for ever, she knew.

She breathed a sigh of relief when Kate's curls appeared around the door.

'Lily!' she exclaimed with a double-take. 'You scared me half to death. What are you doing here?'

The blunt words were muffled as her face was trapped in a cloud of curly hair and she was squeezed in a tight hug.

Pulling back, Kate held her at arm's distance as she gave her an assessing look.

'Of course you're here—stupid of me. How are you doing?' she asked, though Lily knew from her tone that she wasn't expecting an answer. 'Not great, I imagine, from everything that I've heard. Rosie okay?'

Lily nodded, unable to speak after being shown such kindness when she'd been expecting the opposite.

'Now, I need coffee, and I need some sort of baked goods, and then we're going to talk,' Kate carried on, steering Lily back into the kitchen and pulling mugs from the cupboard as the kettle came to the boil. 'That brother of mine has been walking around with a face like a month of wet Sundays, and you're not looking much better yourself. And as it seems like neither of you knows how to operate a telephone or carry out a conversation—despite you having clocked up almost sixty years on this planet between you—an intervention is required.'

Lily dropped onto a stool and opened her mouth to speak.

But Kate stopped her with a pointed finger. 'Uh-uh. I'm talking first. You're sitting like a good girl and listening while I tell you just why *you're* an idiot for pushing my brother away, and *he's* an idiot for letting you and for somehow managing to screw up a romantic whirlwind trip to Rome. And then you're *both* going to apologise and find a way to make this work before your twin glum faces drive me mad. Am I clear?'

Lily didn't know what else to do but nod and accept the coffee that Kate placed in front of her, some of the hot black liquid sloshing over the side of her cup with her enthusiasm.

Despite her rousing sentiments, and her insistence on speaking first, Kate sat and listened quietly as Lily gave her a summed-up version of what had happened in Rome—skirting very quickly round the 'sex with your brother' part and instead focussing on the 'thinking we were falling for each other and then he freaked out and left' part.

Not for the first time she wished she could have fallen for someone else—anyone other than her best friend's brother. Maybe then she could have just spilled out all her worst pain, everything Nic had done wrong, every way he had hurt her and upset her. But knowing how much Kate loved him, how much she knew that he was really a good guy, she couldn't do it.

She couldn't explain what had happened without seeing for herself how much responsibility they both carried for the way things had fallen apart. No, Nic *shouldn't* have left with barely a word the morning after they had made love for the first time. But she should have given him the space he'd needed. Recognised that grieving was a long process, full of setbacks and surprises. That he must have been as taken aback by the turn of events that morning as she had.

And she couldn't deny that pushing him away when he must have been every bit as frightened for Rosie as she had been had been cruel. She just hoped that it wasn't unforgivable.

'So you're both idiots—that's what you're telling me?'

Once again Kate had managed to find a way to compress their entire torturous, complicated lives into one simple sentence.

Lily nodded. 'Though I'm pretty sure I'm the bigger one.'

'You both want to make this up. You're both sitting at home moping rather than doing something about it. Seems pretty equal to me. You know that he wouldn't leave the hospital, right? Slept that first night across a couple of chairs in the A&E waiting room? It wasn't until you texted me that Rosie was fine and I passed it on to him that he would leave. He wanted to be there… just in case.'

Lily dropped her head into her hands, her heart swelling and breaking a little at the same time, ashamed of the way she had behaved, but pleased at this demonstration of Nic's commitment to her—and to Rosie.

'So what do I do about it?'

'Do you want him back? Really?'

She was surprised Kate could ask her that after everything that had just been said—after she'd explained how much she felt for him, how stupid she had been. But in the words she could hear more than a hint of sisterly protection, and Lily knew that she was crossing some sort of rubicon. Say yes now and she wasn't just committing to Nic, she was committing to his family. She was promising not one but two of the people she cared for most in the world that she was committed to them, that she wouldn't hurt them.

'I do,' she said seriously. 'I want us to try again.'

Kate leaned over and gave her a hug with uncharacteristic gentleness, both in her body and her words. 'Glad to hear it. Now, you go borrow my room and get some sleep—you look hideous—and we'll talk again tomorrow.'

Lily felt her body growing heavier. The lack of sleep these past days was catching up with her, and she knew that Kate was right. She needed rest, needed to recharge. And then, when Rosie was better, she'd call Nic, beg his forgiveness, and see if there was any way to rescue what they had so briefly found in Rome.

A few days later Lily reached across to the coffee table, trying to grab her phone without disturbing Rosie, who was asleep on her lap.

It was a message from Kate.

I have a plan. I'll be home in an hour—make sure you're in.

Lily glanced down at the sleeping baby and thought for the millionth time how lucky she was to have her safe and well in her arms—the doctors had given her a clean bill of health, her temperature was gone, and she was feeding and sleeping as normal. The only reason she was being cuddled to sleep instead of drifting off on her own in her cot was because Lily was still nervous of letting her go, still haunted by her worst fears.

It was how Nic must feel every day, she thought, unable to shake the unease of knowing how easily a child could be lost, how impossible it would be to fill the void she would leave.

The doorbell rang, and Lily softly cursed Kate. How could a grown woman, a successful barrister, forget her own house keys on a daily basis?

She set Rosie down, careful not to wake her, and picked her way across the living room. She threw open the door, and had already half turned back when she realised what was wrong with the scene. Kate's slight shoulders wouldn't block the sunshine, wouldn't cast a shadow that was solid and masculine and...

'Nic?'

CHAPTER SIXTEEN

'HI.'

In that moment he knew he'd done the right thing: 'borrowing' his sister's phone, sending that text, coming to see her. Her voice brought memories flooding back…their one night in Rome, their walks around the city, the way she'd heard him confess his darkest fears about his character and told him that she still trusted him. What they'd found together was too important to let it go without a fight.

But maybe Lily was tired of fighting. She looked tired: black bags under her eyes, her shirt unironed, her skin pale. But none of that mattered. Because all he could see was what made her beautiful to him.

How had they managed to get it all so wrong? He thought back to that night in Rome—he couldn't even remember how long ago that was. Four nights? Five? It felt like a lifetime… Everything had seemed right with the world. He'd had the woman he loved, relaxed and happy and contented in his arms. He'd felt peaceful at last, after a decade of running from his memories.

And then in a half waking moment of confusion he'd pushed her away. That one push had spiralled and had a butterfly effect on everything—until he hadn't even recognised who they were to each other any more.

He'd been in so much pain—watching her suffer, watching Rosie suffer—and utterly paralysed with fear that he would lose them both. He should have argued when she'd told him that she wanted to face it alone. Should have told her that he *knew* this pain, *knew* this fear, and that they would be stronger if they faced it together. All he'd been able to do was wait, haunt the hospital waiting room until he'd known that Rosie was going to be okay.

'Come in,' she said, though her voice was hesitant.

He followed her through to the kitchen anyway. He couldn't bear the thought of leaving without things between them being back where they had been. Without her knowing what he'd realised as he'd sat in the hospital, waiting for news, wanting to be nearby just in case she needed him. He loved her. That was why he hadn't been able to go home to his huge, empty apartment. It was why his heart had felt empty for days— why he hadn't been able to sleep or think straight until he'd made the decision to come here and fight for what he wanted. He just hoped it was what she wanted too.

He took a moment to watch her, to refamiliarise himself with her features, with the colour of her hair, the line of her nose and the angle of her smile. Did she know how much he had missed her? How he had missed Rosie as well? Missed the mess and the noise of the two of them at home?

Lily was hovering by the table, and he realised that in his eagerness to look at them both he'd not yet spoken. She looked uncertain, as if she might bolt at any moment, and with that his anger towards her dissipated.

He'd been furious for a while that she wouldn't even answer his texts, that she had left him sitting and wondering whether Rosie was even alive, but seeing her now, seeing the evidence of the emotional toll of the past few days, he found that he couldn't add his anger to her list of troubles.

'The text was from you?' she asked, her voice tremulous.

'I wasn't sure you'd see me. I'm sorry.'

'I would have,' she said. 'I wanted to call…to talk. But after the way I behaved I…I couldn't.'

'You *could*,' he told her. 'That's what you've been trying to show me, isn't it? That we should be finding ways to support each other? I'd have supported you, Lily, if you'd let me. So how is she?' he asked at last, and suddenly his arms felt empty, light, as if they needed the weight of the baby in them to know that she was okay.

Lily wasn't the only one who'd become part of his heart, and he knew that could never be undone.

Never mind his arms, his heart had felt empty these last few days, missing its other half, missing that which made him whole. At first he'd thought it was just the memories making him sad—the thought of another funeral, another tiny white coffin. But when the feeling had persisted long after he'd known that Rosie was in the clear he'd known there was another cause.

Knowing how that felt, knowing what it was to be without her, it suddenly seemed stupid of him to be angry, to hold a grudge. Why jeopardise this? Why risk the chance of being happy?

He met her eyes and tried to show her everything with that look. Everything that he had felt and thought and hoped and feared since he'd last seen her. But it wasn't enough. He had to be sure that she understood.

'I'm sorry,' he said. 'I'm sorry for leaving that morning. I'm sorry that you didn't think you could rely on me when Rosie was sick. I'm sorry it's taken me all week for us to get to this point. I love you, Lily, and I want us to fix this.'

She stared at him for a moment. He wasn't sure what she'd been expecting, but it was clear from her expression that it hadn't been this.

'*I'm* the one who should be apologising,' she said. 'I shouldn't have judged you so harshly when we were in Rome. I shouldn't have pushed you away when Rosie was sick because I was still angry with you.'

'You don't have to apologise,' he said, reaching for her hand and allowing himself a small smile when she didn't pull back. 'You were so worried about her—you had to do what you thought was right at the time.'

'It doesn't make the way I acted any better.'

Nic shrugged. 'We can't change what happened—what we said or did. But if you still want to we can forgive each other. See if we can try harder, do better.'

She smiled, although it still looked tentative. 'I'd like that.'

'I can't promise that I won't have another day like that one in Rome,' he warned. 'There will be times when I feel sad. When I look at Rosie and remember Max. Things might not be smooth sailing just because we want them to be.'

Lily nodded. 'And I can't promise I'm not going to make mistakes, either. It's quite a lot to get used to, this parenting thing. I might need help. Sometimes I might need space.'

'I *can* promise that I will always love you, though. That I will always want you—want you both—in my life.'

'Then I can promise to remember that. Even when I'm upset and angry. I love you, Nic.'

A tear sneaked from the corner of her eye and he reached out with his thumb to wipe it away. The last tear she would shed over him, he hoped.

Rosie started to stir in the bedroom and Nic smiled. 'Can I?' he asked.

Lily nodded and he went to pick the baby up, moved himself beside Lily on the sofa.

'She's really okay?' he asked.

'Right as rain. They were just being cautious. Absolutely the right thing, of course. But it did give me seventy-two hours I'd very much like to wipe from my memory.'

'Just as long as she's okay. And as long as *we* are.'

He placed a tentative arm around her shoulders and his whole body relaxed when she turned into him, burying her face in his neck for a long moment and taking a deep breath. He wished they were at home, that there wasn't a chance his sister might walk through the door at any moment.

Taking advantage of the privacy, temporary as it might be, he dropped a kiss on the top of Lily's head. When she looked up at him he caught her lips with his, holding her there in a long kiss, pouring all the emotion of the last week into it. She moaned as she opened her mouth, and he sensed her longing, her love for him.

As they leaned back in the sofa, nestling together, their little family of three, a thought came to him— and a question...

EPILOGUE

LILY LOOKED IN the mirror. As with pretty much everything else in her life, this wasn't exactly what she'd had in mind. She had always thought she would walk down the aisle on her wedding day looking like something out of one of those bridal magazines. She had never expected to do it eight months pregnant.

The day she'd found out she was expecting their baby had been one of the happiest of their lives. But when they'd sat down and worked out the due date they'd realised that, as always, things were a little complicated. The church and the venue had been booked, and everything had been planned for months. It had seemed silly and vain to change the date of their wedding just so that Lily could buy a gown in the size that she wanted.

After the briefest knock on the door Kate appeared, Rosie propped on one hip and a grin on her face. 'How's the blushing bride getting on?' she asked. 'Better than my brother, I hope. The poor guy's so nervous he can't even eat. Don't know what he's worrying about, personally. Not like you can run very fast in your condition. If you tried to ditch him he'd catch up with you and drag you back.'

'And hi to you too.' Lily laughed, accepting a glass of something sparkling and a kiss on the cheek. 'I'm fine. Better than fine. I'm flippin' brilliant and I cannot wait to be officially your sister. How long have I got?'

Kate checked the time on her phone. 'Three minutes. Right—have we got everything? Old, new, borrowed, blue?'

Lily nodded. Not that she needed any of those things. As long as she had her family she had everything she wanted.

'Let's get you hitched, then.'

She walked into the church and saw Nic waiting for her at the end of the aisle. Any nerves she might have been hiding fell away. She had never felt so happy and in love and safe and secure in her life.

As she turned to look at her guests she saw Helen in the second row, a tissue pressed to her eyes. Her sister looked well, *really* well, better than she'd seen her for a long time. She was making tentative steps to get to know Rosie, and focussing on looking after her own health.

Rosie, still in Kate's arms, went ahead of her up the aisle, so when she reached Nic her little family was all together. Looking around her, Lily felt more lucky than she ever had, and knew as she said 'I do' that nothing could make this moment more perfect.

* * * * *

MILLS & BOON®
Hardback – September 2015

ROMANCE

MILLS & BOON®
Large Print – September 2015

ROMANCE

The Sheikh's Secret Babies	Lynne Graham
The Sins of Sebastian Rey-Defoe	Kim Lawrence
At Her Boss's Pleasure	Cathy Williams
Captive of Kadar	Trish Morey
The Marakaios Marriage	Kate Hewitt
Craving Her Enemy's Touch	Rachael Thomas
The Greek's Pregnant Bride	Michelle Smart
The Pregnancy Secret	Cara Colter
A Bride for the Runaway Groom	Scarlet Wilson
The Wedding Planner and the CEO	Alison Roberts
Bound by a Baby Bump	Ellie Darkins

HISTORICAL

A Lady for Lord Randall	Sarah Mallory
The Husband Season	Mary Nichols
The Rake to Reveal Her	Julia Justiss
A Dance with Danger	Jeannie Lin
Lucy Lane and the Lieutenant	Helen Dickson

MEDICAL

Baby Twins to Bind Them	Carol Marinelli
The Firefighter to Heal Her Heart	Annie O'Neil
Tortured by Her Touch	Dianne Drake
It Happened in Vegas	Amy Ruttan
The Family She Needs	Sue MacKay
A Father for Poppy	Abigail Gordon

MILLS & BOON®
Hardback – October 2015

ROMANCE

Claimed for Makarov's Baby	Sharon Kendrick
An Heir Fit for a King	Abby Green
The Wedding Night Debt	Cathy Williams
Seducing His Enemy's Daughter	Annie West
Reunited for the Billionaire's Legacy	Jennifer Hayward
Hidden in the Sheikh's Harem	Michelle Conder
Resisting the Sicilian Playboy	Amanda Cinelli
The Return of Antonides	Anne McAllister
Soldier, Hero...Husband?	Cara Colter
Falling for Mr December	Kate Hardy
The Baby Who Saved Christmas	Alison Roberts
A Proposal Worth Millions	Sophie Pembroke
The Baby of Their Dreams	Carol Marinelli
Falling for Her Reluctant Sheikh	Amalie Berlin
Hot-Shot Doc, Secret Dad	Lynne Marshall
Father for Her Newborn Baby	Lynne Marshall
His Little Christmas Miracle	Emily Forbes
Safe in the Surgeon's Arms	Molly Evans
Pursued	Tracy Wolff
A Royal Temptation	Charlene Sands

MILLS & BOON®
Large Print – October 2015

ROMANCE

The Bride Fonseca Needs	Abby Green
Sheikh's Forbidden Conquest	Chantelle Shaw
Protecting the Desert Heir	Caitlin Crews
Seduced into the Greek's World	Dani Collins
Tempted by Her Billionaire Boss	Jennifer Hayward
Married for the Prince's Convenience	Maya Blake
The Sicilian's Surprise Wife	Tara Pammi
His Unexpected Baby Bombshell	Soraya Lane
Falling for the Bridesmaid	Sophie Pembroke
A Millionaire for Cinderella	Barbara Wallace
From Paradise...to Pregnant!	Kandy Shepherd

HISTORICAL

A Mistress for Major Bartlett	Annie Burrows
The Chaperon's Seduction	Sarah Mallory
Rake Most Likely to Rebel	Bronwyn Scott
Whispers at Court	Blythe Gifford
Summer of the Viking	Michelle Styles

MEDICAL

Just One Night?	Carol Marinelli
Meant-To-Be Family	Marion Lennox
The Soldier She Could Never Forget	Tina Beckett
The Doctor's Redemption	Susan Carlisle
Wanted: Parents for a Baby!	Laura Iding
His Perfect Bride?	Louisa Heaton

MILLS & BOON®

Why shop at millsandboon.co.uk?

Each year, thousands of romance readers find their perfect read at millsandboon.co.uk. That's because we're passionate about bringing you the very best romantic fiction. Here are some of the advantages of shopping at www.millsandboon.co.uk:

* **Get new books first**—you'll be able to buy your favourite books one month before they hit the shops

* **Get exclusive discounts**—you'll also be able to buy our specially created monthly collections, with up to 50% off the RRP

* **Find your favourite authors**—latest news, interviews and new releases for all your favourite authors and series on our website, plus ideas for what to try next

* **Join in**—once you've bought your favourite books, don't forget to register with us to rate, review and join in the discussions

Visit **www.millsandboon.co.uk**
for all this and more today!